Francis Mansfield

The Gathered Waifs

Containing Lyrics and Odes, Patriotic, Martial and Religious

Francis Mansfield

The Gathered Waifs
Containing Lyrics and Odes, Patriotic, Martial and Religious

ISBN/EAN: 9783744783033

Printed in Europe, USA, Canada, Australia, Japan

Cover: Foto ©Andreas Hilbeck / pixelio.de

More available books at **www.hansebooks.com**

THE GATHERED WAIFS:

CONTAINING LYRICS AND ODES
PATRIOTIC, MARTIAL, AND
RELIGIOUS.

BY

Dr. S. D. LEIFSNAM,

NEW YORK:
1898.

Respectfully Dedicated to the Members

of the

U. S. Grant Post, No. 327, G. A. R.,

of Brooklyn, N. Y.,

By their Comrade, the Author.

150 NASSAU STREET,
  NEW YORK CITY,
    JUNE 1, 1898.

CONTENTS.

CONTENTS.

APOLOGIA.

Go, precious Book, condemned to moderate praise,
Or worse, to words with barbarous censure fraught;
Enter, with modest mien, the poor man's cot,
To crown his features with a wreath of smiles;
Or spread thy pages in the halls of kings,
From royal eyes to press a regal tear.
When thou art humbled with neglect and scorn,
Think of the thousand books which shared thy fate.
When critics, hissing with envenomed sting,
Strike with their poison fangs through ribs of steel
To reach thy throbbing heart, heed not their thrust,
Though angrily they tear thee into shreds,
And spare thee not from spoliation dire,
Nor save one fragment from pollution's stain.
How many a book's like thee condemned to wait,
Its author living haply in mean repute,
"Damned to faint praise," yet, after his decease,
Though crushed to earth, is nobly doomed to rise,
Soar on immortal wings through sunlit skies,
Whose fame's eternal as heaven's blest abode,
Where dwell the souls whose deeds were wondrous fair.
Since flattery aims to compass with false praise,
Then cease thy fawning on the world's great sons, —
(Pardon the word; there is none great but God).

Paint thy rough cheek with modesty's fair blush,
While stationed near the masters of Greek verse,
And, to the charm of more pretentious song,
Yield diadems to Poesy's bright fame.
Thou hadst no patron to thy pastoral lay;
No rich Mecænas plumed thy wings for flight.
And shouldst thou fail to reach Parnassus' height,
Or snowy summit of Olympus, where
The gods bestow immortal wreaths and crowns,
Remember that thine infancy was bred
Far from the gushing of Pierian springs.
What pride we 'd take, what noble joy and bliss,
To see thee marching down the centuries
Linked arm in arm with Byron, Gray, or Moore;
Or to behold thee sharing thy meed of note
With Homer, Milton, Shakespeare, like the host
Of nature's peerless bards who won earth's fame.
Go, little Waifs, scattered like autumn leaves,
Through hoary frost and winter's cold outspread,
'Twixt heaven and earth, the living and the dead,—
Win your first laurels from the tented field,
Where our brave warriors waved victorious swords.
When round the world ye trace your trackless course,
In future years, return once more and tell
How eagerly men sought " The Gathered Waifs."
Go forth, thou wanderer o'er the pathless deep,
Like the bold seaboy cradled on its waves;
Sail to the harbor where the solemn priest

Swings censers facing some Egyptian god,
And watch the incense in the Ephesian fane
Rise to the top of yon cathedral dome.
Haste to the forest and Hyrcanian wilds,
Where greedy wolves devour defenceless lambs;
Go, like the troubadour or wandering Jew,
Search out the beggar in his bed of straw,
Where Islam wields his simitar of steel, —
The Orient hospice shelters homeless guest;
Or perish in the pit of horrid Robur,
Like brave Jugurtha, hurled to traitor's doom.
Go, thou Iconoclast, through Folly's land,
And smite the idols of the human mind;
The superstitious age of ignorance
Hath set her images upon the shrine
Of Giaour's devotions; tear them rudely down,
From dusty niches in their temple walls.
Spare faith in Jesus; make the bold attempt
To fix Christ's statue on his pedestal.
Seek lore from Moab's stone and Dighton rock;
Rehearse the cabalistic formula;
Transmute base metals into solid gold,
Base deeds of men to virtue by the power
Of stone yclept philosophers of yore.
Go forth, grim as the pallid face of Death,
To yonder peak where dwells the mystic sage,
And summon Delphic oracles to prove
By auguries the phantom of thy dreams.

Plumed like the knight in martial splendor clad,
Drive thy swift steeds along the Appian Way;
Then pause a while beyond the Roman walls
At Virgil's tomb; there rest thy chariot-wheels;
Revere the honored dead and haste away,
Until the tocsin sounds in carnival.
When nature spreads before thy ravished gaze,
The alluring prospect of autumnal fields,
Stroll on the bank of lake and dancing brooks,
Among the reeds and rushes in the woods;
There find thy solace, and the healing balm,
Since hostile arrows pierced thy bubbly pride.
Then, after all thy journeys through the wilds,
Return once more unto thy cherished friends,
To comforts and the cheerful voice of song,
By the fireside of thine own New England home.
Time is not ripe yet for thy poet's fame;
Some future century will own his worth.
After one thousand years have sped away,
It shall be proved thine author wrote no verse,
But Bacon's genius wrought thy senseless rhymes.
When vampire critics threat with evil eye
To shut the gates of doom against the soul,
Skate thou along the spider's brittle thread,
Above the gates of hell, o'er fiery flood,
Through yonder portals, to those distant realms,
Where Moslem houris wait in Paradise.

SLEEP.

The lingering moon, which mounts the starlit dome,
  Looks through the clefts of yonder fleecy cloud,
To light belated travellers journeying home,
  Or watch men sleeping in their nightly shroud.

The evening air which glides so calm and still,
  Yet breathes in gentle whispers through the trees,
Soothes the hot brow of maidens who are ill,
  Who bless the soft, kind nursing of the breeze.

O slumber, come and seal these drooping eyes;
  Cradle this brain in that soft couch of thine;
Compose these weary limbs in death's disguise;
  Sprinkle this brow with dew of anodyne.

Let no rough sound, and no corroding cares,
  Disturb these calm, serene, and peaceful dreams,
No rude alarms assail, till morning dares
  To mock night's goddess with her golden beams.

LIFE'S LIGHT AND SHADOW.

On land and ocean, through severe constraint,
  How vast the number who but watch and weep;
The wretched suffer, weary hearts grow faint,
  While we, their fellow-mortals, idly sleep.

While brave men rest, tyrants bear cruel sway,
  And crush the cowards down like abject slaves;
Then, Patriots, rise, on Liberty's bright day,
  And hurl all despots to their doom, their graves!

Rich, proud, and great, they drive their chariot-wheels
  Along the boulevard, in matchless style;
But modest peasants toil in fallow fields,
  Like negroes on the borders of the Nile.

Hear Ramah's children, crying for their bread,
  Their mother weeping, that she's none to give;
In their hard lot, 't were better to be dead
  Than thus in starving wretchedness to live.

The ancient grandam whirls her buzzing wheel,
    With pinioned distaff to her bodice pressed,
Spins gold or silver thread, and turns her reel,
    Weaves wizard's doublet, as beseems her best.

The brightest days and darkest nights pass by,
    As oft the rolling tides both flow and ebb ;
As swift as shuttles, busy moments fly,
    With warp and woof, to form life's tangled web.

From all the past, where we once dropped our tears,
    Lost on oblivion's blank and silent page,
Forward we gaze, through dark and misty years,
    Toward yonder goal which bounds life's tragic stage.

The clouds which shadow life above us loom,
    But all the sky their silver linings fill,
Whose radiance, lighting and dispelling gloom,
    Tells us that yonder sun is shining still.

Beneath the blackness of a lowering sky,
    The frown of Deity inflicts a smart, —
Hath Heaven no alchemy to cure a sigh,
    No antidote to heal a bleeding heart?

When all is bright, within life's glorious prime,
    Before the days of darkness and of gloom,
The voice, still blending with melodious chime,
    Retains its strength, the cheek its youthful bloom.

When manhood's strength has bent to hoary years,
    The power is gone, which won this world's renown;
Man vents his grief in sorrow's bitter tears,
    Like some proud czar, robbed of his regal crown.

Man's earthly life is never all a cloud,
    But through the rift, the sunlight often cheers;
Though night be dark, and covered with a shroud,
    All earth is bright when dawning day appears.

How dark it seems within the vaulted cave!
    How sad the hour of man's departing breath!
How dismal is the clod which lines the grave,
    Within the vale and shade of ghastly death!

High Heaven provides a rest for human ills,
    And spreads the bow of promise after storms,
Above the summits of those rugged hills,
    Where drops the tinted rain in piebald forms.

Why art thou pensive, O my downcast soul?
    Cease thy sad plaint, although thy heart be sore,
While through yon cloud fond memory bids the scroll
    Portray the face which thou canst see no more.

Some toil and weep, while others rest or laugh,
    They vainly struggle, they can do no more;
While princes from their cups potations quaff,
    Slaves bear torn hearts, sprinkled with blood and gore.

While some in joy, yet more in travail tread
    The lonesome path, along life's toilsome road;
Sometimes by vice, anon by virtue led,
    They fall beneath the burden of their load.

When wearily alone, 'neath murky dome,
    Along the rugged wild, o'er thorny path,
The wayworn pilgrim strays afar from home,—
    His bosom swells with bitterness of wrath.

The lurid light, through rifts of dark gray cloud,
    Reveals the storm in his tempestuous soul;
With anguish tossed, he lifts his voice aloud,
    And cries to Heaven for help, while thunders roll.

Sometimes repining in the summer heat,
  Or in biting sharpness of the wintry cold,
When pinched with hunger, chilled with snow and sleet,
  He suffers pain and miseries untold.

'T is grateful for each traveller to learn,
  Howe'er his journey ends, though deep his grave,
His ashes, stored within earth's sacred urn,
  Shall, phœnix-like, arise from land or wave.

How sad it seems to be thus left alone,
  Bereft of friends, and weary of this life!
But winds may waft his sighs to worlds unknown,
  Where Pity crowns the slave of toil and strife.

Take courage, noble, weak, and weary heart,
  Beyond heaven's wicket, I can faintly see;
However rough may be thine earthly part,
  Beyond death's portal, there is joy for thee.

On yonder hill, the cottage roofed with thatch,
  Stands buttressed with heaven's choice of fragrant
      vine;
Approach the gate, and gently lift the latch,
  The warm embrace of welcome shall be thine.

Kinsfolk in youth, who reached there long before,
   Await thy coming on those heights above;
Whole groups of friends, around the latticed door,
   Still proffer tokens of enduring love.

Through mist and mazes of a way obscure,
   Each setting sun reveals the shadowed gloam;
Less human sadness hast thou to endure,
   One wayside milestone nearer to thy home.

THE SOLDIER'S RECOMPENSE.

Decorum est pro Patria mori.

In bright array, the hostile phalanx fought,
   With bayonet and sabre cut their way;
So wide and deep, the havoc which they wrought,
   That, felled to earth, ten thousand warriors lay.

Lo, here, how dreadful these sad fruits of war!
   Men groaning, dying, strewn along the plain;
When ceased the battle, their brave comrades saw
   A piteous sight, the wounded, bleeding, slain.

Sigh not for these alone; for oft, I ween,
   Still sorer griefs attend the slaughtered brave;
Lift up the veil, and view the distant scene,
   Where tears are falling on that soldier's grave.

Can all the glory of a kingly crown;
   Can splendid mounds, or monuments of art;
The fame of conquest, victor's high renown, —
   Check sorrow's stream which flows through one sad
      heart?

Through years of anguish, must these sorrows last,
  The field of carnage fills the earth with dread;
Remembrance hovers round the awful past, —
  Millions are mourning still their absent dead.

The warrior welcomes death, if he may free
  His native land, or country's life may save;
The nation's gain is marked, where freedom's tree
  Takes root in every patriot hero's grave.

Commend the care of each brave soul to God,
  His corse and tomb bid every people prize;
Let fadeless flowers blossom o 'er the sod,
  Above his mound, let cloud-capped columns rise.

The price of freedom, who can fully know,
  Or worth of valor in her holy cause?
With laurel wreath, we crown the victor's brow;
  The world his courage cheers, with rapt applause.

All men behold heroic deeds with pride,
  The heavens bend over with majestic awe,
The sun itself dispels, and scatters wide
  The gruesome gloom, the dark, grim dearth of war.

What coins of gold comprise the soldier's fee?
　　What boon can balance all his mortal groans?
War breaks the bondman's chain, sets captives free;
　　War crushes empires, and shakes tyrants' thrones.

To freedom, peace and home, what debts we owe!
　　Columbia's land, home of the noble free!
Thrice have thine armies vanquished every foe,
　　Thy navies thrice have swept him from the sea.

Columbia's flag has stars not dimmed nor lost,
　　But clearer, brighter shine they every year,
Till soon, in numbers vast as swell the host
　　Of heaven, their splendid beauty shall appear.

Armies and hosts, so vast and without number;
　　Navies and fleets that never more shall roam;
Nations of men whose bodies lie in slumber, —
　　All gather on the journey toward their home.

The heavens throw wide the everlasting portals,
　　While hope invites to pleasures yet unseen,
Save by the sense of happiest immortals,
　　Who rove those hills and pastures ever green.

Think, in that country pleasure has no end;
  Gladness, contentment, come alike to all;
The soul rejoices, evil has no friend,
  Hearts have no sorrow, eyes no tears to fall.

Talk not of earthly beauty, vernal flowers,
  Of fields where waving grasses strew the plain,
Or gardens rich with perfume, wet with showers,
  Nor boast of rose-beds washed with gentle rain.

The fairest scenes that Nature yet hath made,
  Stretch far away beyond the deep blue sky.
Behold the land where flowers never fade,
  Where roses bloom, and blossoms never die.

There mansions stand, wreathed in immortal vine,
  Whose tendrils cling to walls of gems and gold;
There bowers extend, decked in sweet eglantine,
  And temples tower in splendor yet untold.

PREPARATION FOR THE CONFLICT.

One fights for conquest, aided by the Fates;
   He thus gains glory to adorn his grave.
Our nation sought reunion of the States,
   And won a benison for every slave.

War hath its grievances and bitter pangs,
   'T is but a monster spread across the way,
That, like a snake with venom in his fangs,
   Strikes to destroy or blight his harmless prey.

The cruelty of war, the poet's theme,
   May kindle in the soul majestic fire;
What else can better serve to deck his dream,
   Or what so well his lofty thought inspire?

Night spreads her sable veil o'er all around;
   The dew distils her gifts with gentle grace;
Stars shed their radiance upon the ground;
   Sleep wraps earth's millions in her soft embrace.

The picket guard stands sentinel till late,
  And paces to and fro in midnight gloom;
No hostile form appears to rouse his hate,
  And all is quiet, — silent as the tomb.

CHRONICLE OF STRUGGLE IN EARLY DAYS.

The portents of impending conflict seemed
To threaten war. For years the prospect gleamed
Bright with the flash of steel, until at last
The war-cloud burst, with sound of bugle's blast.

The threat of war then clouds the Southern sky,
And proud Rebellion lifts her banners high,
Flings down the gauntlet at Fort Sumpter's walls, —
The nation totters when the fortress falls.

Now Congress moves for war, with dread alarms,
While Lincoln calls Columbia to arms;
Soon three-score thousand men confront the foe,
Whom rebel legions strive to overthrow.

Their country calls men, and they must obey,
Their duty summons them in haste away;
To patriots and to this time belong
Historic deeds, made memorable in song.

Far o'er the land now rests a gloomy cloud,
Like darkest midnight veiled in dismal cloud;
The timid women tremble, brave men quail,
Through fear that valor now will not avail.

See broad, expansive earth begirt with sky;
See wide encircling dome hung up on high;
Where camp-fires blaze at night beneath the stars,
And cannon shake the earth like pagan Mars.

The day is bright in autumn sixty-two
When marching orders come for grand review;
Men brandish bayonets and sabres wield,
And catch the foe feagued on the bloody field.

The hostile camp is pitched before the dawn,
While trumpet notes salute the coming morn;
Ere yet the darkness has quite passed away,
The cannon roar to greet the break of day.

The warlike squadrons marshalled on the plain
Commence to slaughter and ignore the slain;
With sabre stroke and clash of sword they kill, —
With musket-balls or grape-shot, as they will.

The smoke of battle in the blaze of war
Casts deep its shade o'er country wide and far;
The ghastly spectacle, pale, silent, dead,
Strikes sorrow to all hearts and thrills with dread.

And as the eagles swoop upon their prey —
Trussing and pluming, bear them swift away —
So they, in majesty and might, pour down
To pounce on armies, and thus win renown.

Behold the frowning aspect of the sky,
The savage hilltops towering up on high!
When gathering clouds predict the wildest storm,
So fatal signs portend death's dreadful form.

When proud battalions speed along the plain,
They march, like steeds whose spirits never wane,
With measured pace, with martial footsteps tread,
Till night's black mantle round their tent is spread.

Soldiers of sterner mettle made than hares
Quail not for stroke which ambushed foeman bears;
They dread no ghost, like cowards seized with fright
When spectres cast grim shadows in the night.

Warriors, compact of steel, and sturdy bred,
Stand proof to flying bullets, hail of lead;
Smell powder's smoke, as hounds scent track of deer;
Rush to the thickest fight, and own no fear.

By cannon's mouth brave soldiers fall and writhe,
Like swaths of grass before the mower's scythe;
Are swallowed up by death on every side,
Like seamen buried in the ocean tide.

Time, marching on with slow, majestic tread,
Conducts man soon to realms which mortals dread:
But battle piles up heaps of slain in hours,
When shot and shell come pouring down in showers.

As Scottish bards their bagpipes tune to drone
To buglers' sound the chord with death's deep groan,
When soldiers falling, pierced with mortal wound,
Lie prostrate, strewn upon the blood-stained ground.

THE WAR FOR THE UNION.

Three hundred thousand men must fly to arms;
   At Lincoln's call our country must be saved!
On land and sea, alive with war's alarms,
   O'er one vast realm, her banner shall be waved!

This mandate reached the nation's utmost bound,
   And patriotic hearts are set on fire.
When duty summons brave men, these have found
   That themes of war can with bold thoughts inspire.

Gird on your swords for battle, ye Brave Chiefs,
   That fought at Palo Alto on the moors!
Strike, to redress your country's bleeding griefs!
   Fight, that this native land may still be yours!

America must liberate her sons,
   And break the shackles from three million slaves,
Whose freedom costs gold eagles weighing tons,
   Countless young lives, and fills a million graves.

And what was worth the treasure and the blood,
　So freely sacrificed at Freedom's shrine?
The gore that streamed like tides upon the flood,
　Bought union for this nation, yours and mine.

Saving our land excelled this princely price;
　Her value equals all our heroes' lives.
No recompense can for her loss suffice;
　They fought for fathers, brothers, children, wives.

OUR FIRST GREAT BATTLE.

Men, in hot haste, were hurrying to and fro,
　And two vast armies stood with angry frown,
Like clouds surcharged with fire, threatening the foe,
　Eager to shoot the hostile squadrons down.

See those black thunderclouds! how fierce they are!
　How menacing they look, while they draw near!
Till, in a moment of suspense, they jar
　The earth as they explode, startling with fear.

Thus do the armies of the North and South,
  Confront opposing forces at Bull Run,
Marshal their columns at the cannon's mouth,
  And struggle, till the battle's lost and won.

The bugle call awakes Virginia's hills,
  And far-resounding echoes reach the plains;
The clash of arms through every bosom thrills,
  And booming cannon tell that battle reigns.

How many a bright and sparkling hope oft springs,
  From the welling fountain of the youthful breast,
When the gate of morn on silver pinion swings,
  The god of day hastes toward the golden west;

But a clouded sun rolls through the murky sky,
  And stamps those prospects with a fearful blight;
In darker hours, then Phœbus mounts on high,
  And sinks at last, to black and dismal night.

So rose the sun upon that glorious day,
  Inspiring hope and gladness like a flood;
How quickly sped those fleeting dreams away!
  That sun went down in sorrow, shame, and blood.

The surging tides of cannon, horse, and men,
   Backward and forward sway, each one in course;
Repulsed, they rally to the charge again,
   And yield no portion to superior force.

With blazing musketry, with shell and ball,
   Those armies fiercely mow each other down,
And who that sees a thousand soldiers fall,
   Will dare deny that each deserves a crown?

The people's hearts with full strong throbbings beat,
   And fiery passions burst the utmost bound;
With flashing eyes, the masses rose to meet
   The peril of the hour, from depths profound.

Alas, for human hopes! how quickly fled!
   The voice of Fate proclaims this sure decree:
The Union stars and stripes shall float o'erhead,
   Till every State sets all her children free.

While pale in death, the bodies strew the plain,
   Their comrades covered them beneath the sod;
With bleeding hearts, these sorrowed for the slain,
   Stood for their country, and firmly trusted God.

With muffled drums, and arms reversed, they tread;
  No funeral dirge nor requiem is heard;
O'er those remains, one simple prayer is said,
  But all our hearts felt sad with that last word.

The soldier needs no casket and no pall,
  But when the noble hero bravely dies,
Who then can count the manly tears that fall,
  Or who restrain his comrades' countless sighs?

Roll on, dark Clouds, that hover o'er these graves,
  And spend your fury in tempestuous gust;
Drop not your waters on the ocean waves,
  But nourish wild flowers o'er this sacred dust.

The man who welcomes death in virtue's cause,
  And for his country, bravely dares to die,
Obeys the dictate of Heaven's wisest laws,
  And shares the fame of realms beyond the sky.

Blest is that land whose sons are true and bold,
  Whose rights the chieftain yields his life to save,
And Mother Earth feels doubly proud to hold
  The priceless treasure of a hero's grave.

Pray, bear his body gently to the tomb,
    Fire your last volley sweetly as you may,
" The lights are out " within his silent room,
    He waits the reveillé of coming day.

When on that morrow, he shall rise at dawn,
    March homeward on the path he never trod;
Who then shall greet him in the early morn? —
    His own dear kindred, his Father and his God.

THE ARMY WAITING FOR ACTION.

The Union army halted with the van,
    As proud as eagles, on their mountain crag;
And rapture seized the heart of every man,
    While Victory was perching on his flag.

The stillness of midnight calmly settles round,
    Serenely there the Union banners wave,
Until the shouting breaks the calm profound,
    On the borderland, where Freedom greets the slave.

Where Taurus rules his native herd of kine,
  King of the pasture, where he reigns supreme,
There two vast armies, drawn in martial line,
  Stand heedless of the ill-omened vulture's scream.

Forebodings, dark and rueful, dwell not where
  The mettle of true valor fills the breast;
The harsh, wild croak of ravens doth not scare
  The man who crushes hydras in their nest.

Within the soldier's heart a cheerful hope
  Yet lingers, when all passions else are fled;
E'en when defeat hath crushed his power to cope,
  A gleam from heaven shines round his radiant head.

The nation's horn of power dwells in her host;
  For strength the army can alone bestow;
And with this mighty arm, she makes her boast
  To crush, destroy, and overwhelm the foe.

Deprived of men, of weapons quite bereft,
  She, like a lion with a toothless jaw,
Can seize no prey, and has no courage left,
  Defenceless as a bear which has no paw.

An army without head is but a mob,
  Which turns against itself in heedless fight,
And spends its force in murdering to rob, —
  But discipline must act with valor's might.

When peaceful measures serve not to repair
  The breach which wise diplomacy ignored,
And arbitration deals with schemes unfair,
  Arbitrament must poise upon the sword.

The wretch who heeds not when his country cries
  To him for help, and summons him afield,
Is named a coward; for mankind despise
  The traitor, whose dishonor stains his shield.

The volunteer, enrolled on page of fame,
  With broad escutcheon and heraldic rhyme,
Shall win his coat-of-arms and honored name,
  For proud posterity through endless time.

Within the sphere of base Desertion's caste,
  What can heroic virtue e'er implant?
How strangely these two characters contrast,
  The traitor Arnold, and the chieftain Grant.

THE ARMY IN BATTLE.

So gallantly they fight on either side,
  In rough environment of hill and vale,
That officers survey the field with pride,
  Mid showers of deadly balls and leaden hail.

They lead the charge; then, driven back by force,
  Renew the eager onset quick and fast,
Till Union troops, masking the battle's course,
  Disperse the rebels' broken ranks at last.

The storm which beats the cloud-capped battle-wall,
  And shrieks for vengeance on the sheltered foe,
Now breaks the ramparts of the castled hall,
  Their fragments o'er the shattered bastions strew.

Ah, what is human life! How small a gift
  To sacrifice on altars of that land
Which gave us birth! Alas! at length how swift
  Life ebbs away within the Maker's hand.

The soldier longs to share the martyr's doom,
 And dreads to weigh his treasures in the scale
Against his country's needs, — nor fears the tomb,
 Where honors lie in Freedom's placid vale.

By Fate's irrevocably firm decree,
 It stands recorded as a truth to warn:
Amid these shifting scenes we shall not be
 Forever; life, like a shadow, soon is gone.

Along the field of battle lie the slain;
 The wounded, bleeding, gasping for their breath,
Lean on their arms in agonizing pain,
 Until set free from suffering by death.

What multitudes on that long muster-roll,
 Join the ascending host that storms the fort
And battlements of heaven, with prayerful soul,
 And entrance gain to that celestial port!

The iron-bound and gallant stout-rigged ships
 Cast anchor for eternity within
The realms of paradise, where man equips
 His brow with laurels which he craved to win.

Think how the brave deserves thy fond caress;
  Nor doth he boast of cruelty alone;
But let each gentle maid with pride confess,
  He has a heart as tender as her own.

Dreaming of home, the soldier often lies
  Outstretched upon the field, both pale and wan;
But when he leads the charge, or wins the prize,
  The love of one sweet damsel leads him on.

He marches proudly to the seat of war,
  And boldly mounts the ramparts of the foe;
Cheered by the voices that resound from far,
  Whose echoes reach the distant plains below.

OUR AMERICAN WAR SONG.

Ducit amor patriae.

Here is death to the traitor who dares to betray;
  But behold, where the hero his standard unfurls!
To the Stars and the Stripes, let the nations give way,
  For our banner leads on to the conquest of worlds.

To the battle, Brave Warriors, display your bold clan!
　In your rage and your fury, still fight as of yore;
Strike the enemy down, till ye slay the last man,
　And then march on in triumph through victory's gore.

In the shock of the breach, we will grapple with steel,
　Till the sabre shall reek with the blood of the slain,
And our swords shall compel them, like vassals, to kneel,
　And to beg their release from captivity's chain.

Let our cannon demolish their breastwork of rock,
　Like an avalanche, crash through the bastion's firm
　　　wall,
Till the mountains shall quake with th' imperious shock,
　And the clouds shall re-echo the blast of their fall.

We shall brook no more boast from an insolent foe,
　But revenge the proud look of contempt and disdain;
We shall hurl back their threats with a gigantic blow,
　And repay their bold insults with torture and pain.

Should oppression and tyranny rise in our land,
　We will drive them to regions below, whence they
　　　came;
Like the patriots of our revolution we'll stand,
　And our sons shall outrival their forefathers' fame.

Over this, our free country, the people hold power,
  If no franchise or ballot, they shall sway with the
    sword.
Let the demagogue tremble and the anarchist cower,
  Since the buzzard feels dazed, where the eagle has
    soared.

When our chivalry marshal their host to a man,
  'Gainst the treacherous hatred and sceptre of Spain,
We shall shame the bold arrogance of haughty Japan,
  And send hope to the islands wherever we reign.

※

THE AMERICAN SOLDIER'S FOND RECOLLECTIONS.

America, my pride, my chiefest joy!
  Oh, all day long my heart is full of glee, —
Where happy days my gladdest thoughts employ, —
  The Yankee boys, they are the boys for me!

Within the soul, their patriot feelings glow
  With aspirations, noble, grand, and true;
They, leading onward, strong against the foe,
  Through fields of danger and of blood, pursue.

Ah, bravest comrades of heroic Giaours!
    We hail your martial prowess with applause;
We honor Spartan valor equal ours,
    Nor less the sires who fell in our great wars.

Proud of my country, while my bosom swells
    To learn some conquest she has won anew,
I hear the spirit's voice which clearly tells,
    "No alien soldiers match the 'boys in blue.'"

In bloody days of "auld lang syne," our sires
    Would crush invaders from beyond the sea;
They kindled sparks to torches, coals to fires,
    And flames to conflagrations wild and free.

Indomitable sires on Bunker Hill,
    Unflinching faced the foe, 'mid cannons' roar, —
There stands the shaft which marks their glory still,
    Intrepid patriots of those days of yore.

No less in fame, their sons of sixty-one
    Marched to the front to heal the nation's woes;
Through four long years, in battles lost and won,
    They fought, and conquered this lorn country's foes.

Intoxicated with the victor's joy,
　　Each soldier stacked his arms 'neath heaven's blue
　　　　dome ;
With parting words and tears from each brave boy,
　　He turned his footsteps towards his own dear home.

His heart and pulse, throbbing with strong desire,
　　Quickened his pace until he reached the door,
Rejoiced to see beside the yew-log fire
　　The maid that he loved best his own once more.

THE FLAG OF OUR UNION.

May the flag of our country henceforth ever bear,
All the stars and the stripes boldly floating in air !
May the star-spangled banner, forever and aye,
Wave her folds of defence, o'er the blue and the gray !

Let the Union of States continue to stand,
And the power of our arms rule the sea and the land,
Till the heavens and the earth become shrouded in
　　　　gloom,
When the ages to come shall have passed to the tomb.

THE WARRIOR'S BRAVERY.

The warrior stern, no waggish snob is he;
  In character, he's manly, bold, and brave;
In manner, courteous, chivalric, and free;
  Prompt to obey commands, and yet no slave.

Inscribed in memory's tablet, names in gold
  Shine through the ages, bright as flaming stars
Fixed in their orbits of cerulean mould,
  Whose meteoric splendor equals Mars.

Proudly across the ramparts of the foe
  They march to conquest with their flags unfurled.
Tumultuous throngs press on to overthrow,
  Whose cannon echo round th' encompassed world.

Pale, ghostlike forms, the swift-winged messengers
  Of heaven, dwell in the clouds above the slain,
And brood around them; not a lone leaf stirs
  Within the wildwood of that templed fane.

While wan the moon paced Zodiac's steep side,
  Beneath the veil of night, their legend saith,
Sleep swept by, like an overwhelming tide,
  And sealed their eyes in miniature of death.

The patriotic warrior fights amain
  For glory less than for his country's weal;
His nation's vantage thus he strives to gain,
  As oft distressed, to Heaven she lifts appeal.

He mounts his steed with falchion by his side,
  And gallops o'er the plain with gallant pace;
Midst bullets thick as rain pursues his ride,
  Nor heeds the ghastly wounds that scar his face.

He climbs the hill, in masterly array,
  Through thicket, tanglewood, o'er ditch and wall;
He leaps from moat to parapet away,
  To fort and garrison, and captures all.

What will the soldier do and bravely dare
  To win his country's generous meed of praise?
He'll face the cannon's mouth with courage rare,
  Wrest victory from the battle's lurid blaze.

With solemn tread, his corse, in silence borne,
  Now rests beneath the willow's sombre shade,
Whom once the muffled drum-beat bade us mourn,
  Beside the shattered bastion's esplanade.

The sister or the sweetheart vents her love
  By sighing out in the cold moonless air;
Breathing her plaints like some sad moaning dove
  That's lost her cooing mate in the fowler's snare.

Thus parent, wife, and brother, sister, friend,
  Vie in their spheres our soldiers' luck to share,
And every patriot will his greeting send,
  For the hardships and the sufferings they bear.

RESULT OF CONFLICT RENEWED.

Meanwhile the battle's din resounds afar;
  The smoke of flashing powder mounts on high;
The cannonade sets rifted rocks ajar,
  Like peals of thunder from the hills and sky.

Hear how the cannon make the welkin ring
 Till earth re-echoes to the ponderous sound.
The shot fly swiftly on electric wing,
 And fell their victims to the blood-stained ground.

The flower of Southern chivalry must yield
 To the virile strength of overwhelming force,
And lose brave comrades on the tented field,
 Since War pursues his ever deadly course.

The strongest column seldom fails to win;
 But numbers do not always furnish might:
In fratricidal strife against our kin
 God helps the cause of Justice, Truth, and Right.

The stirring notes of bugle, fife, and drum,
 Of clarion horn that summons to the fray,
Shall rouse stern courage in the hearts of some,
 With valiant deeds to gain the doubtful day.

Intrepid warriors from a knightly clan,
 Arrayed in steel, with armor to defend,
Yet need a Chief superior to man,
 Wisdom to guide and valor to contend.

Proudly they marched toward their palatial home
With that grand army which enlists the soul;
At night some slept beneath the spangled dome
Whose names at morn stood on life's muster-roll.

No dreams can now disturb the peaceful breast;
They long ago have reached the distant shore
Where the patriot, valiant soldier finds his rest,
Where the bugle or the drum-beat calls no more.

The buried dead, how calm and still they lie!
Reposing sweetly in a soldier's grave;
No clarion trump now swells the quiet sky,
To herald deeds of glory by the brave.

THE END OF WAR APPROACHING.

Where the sweet rose, and lily white as snow,
Scatter perfumes through the air unto the sky,
On the border land of Dixie, stood the foe,
Just where the blooming heather greets the eye.

But the roses, frightened at the sight of blood,
   Have ever since grown pale upon the vine;
They blanch their color in the early bud,
   Although of yore they blushed as red as wine.

No Union soldier's cheek e'er blanched with fear,
   But many a face in death grew pale and cold
(When cowards fall no soldier sheds a tear);
   But rebel warriors matched ours quite as bold.

The sword hath power the bond to disenthral,
   And boldly thwart the traitor's deeds of shame;
In matchless valor one surpasses all;
   And maidens vie to sing this chieftain's name;

For when the Union cause seemed nearly lost,
   In that dark hour of solemn midnight gloom,
The ship was wildly drifting tempest-tossed,
   He seized the helm and stayed her threatened doom.

As Cæsar crossed the Rubicon, and bore
   The Roman eagles through the Appian way,
Thus o'er the grim Potomac's hostile shore
   Grant raised our banner where it waves to-day.

The foe disputed every rood of ground,
   And gave fierce battle in the Wilderness;
At length our army compassed them around
   With high intrenchments, and with stern duress.

From every quarter of the heavens men came, —
   East, North, and West, the mountains and the sea;
Wherever heroes then deserved the name
   They swelled the host that set our bondmen free.

Bestow thy thought upon that anxious throng
   Who sit in pensive grief and tears at home;
Whose hearts transfixed with many a painful thong
   Yearn for the boys in gray where'er they roam.

A father waits your last report to learn,
   Stops in the furrow, leans upon his plough, —
Oh, tell the sire his son shall soon return,
   Wreaths on his hand and laurel on his brow!

The mother sits in gloomy solitude,
   Spends sleepless nights in longing for her child;
Dreams he is lost within some tangled wood,
   Or sees his mangled form in forest wild.

When borne on stretcher from the battlefield,
　Wounded in bloody limbs and racked with pain,
What rapture doth anticipation yield
　The thought that he'll soon reach his home again!

The South choose union stripes in place of bars,
　Transform their uniforms of gray to blue,
Restore old flags with all their lustrous stars,
　Change thought and heart from false intent to true.

Beneath the shade of yonder gnarled oak,
　Which stands upon the hillside there alone,
The wounded soldier lies, felled by the stroke
　Of some sharp cutlass piercing to the bone.

His pensiveness alternates with good cheer,
　Between the thoughts of home and stinging pain;
His whispered meditations pierce our ear
　While he mutters some old poem's sweet refrain.

THE BATTLEFIELD AFTER THE CONFLICT.

Beneath the canopy of heaven's blue dome,
  The smoke of battle had just cleared away;
The evening twilight darkened into gloam;
  On the dewy grass our wounded comrades lay.

The moon's pale beams fell on each anxious brow,
  Revealing pain and anguish pictured there;
Heaven heard intently many a sacred vow,
  And prayer beseeching God's paternal care.

That night the angel of the sable wing
  Was brooding in the air above the slain,
Choosing his victims, like a mighty king
  Swaying his sceptre o'er the bloody plain.

The mortal shaft, well-aimed at vital part,
  Fell deadly on the wounded soldier's frame,
And stayed his panting breath and beating heart,
  And stopped his throbbing pulse with ruthless shame.

Right upward, through th' ethereal, brilliant dome,
  The soul, emancipated, winged his flight
To paradise, his own celestial home,
  Whose beauty captivates the ravished sight.

The pomp and pageantry of earth no more
  Attracts the gaze or wins the heart of men
Whose pallid faces, sprinkled with red gore,
  Look upward towards that land which bounds their ken.

Sad as the melancholy tomb, that field
  Lies shrouded in the sombre veil of night;
With death's dark pall the gloomy view is sealed
  Till the morrow's sun breaks o'er the ghastly sight.

The battlefield, with wounded and the slain,
  More frightful than a charnel-house of bones,
Appeals to man's deep sympathy for pain, —
  O'er fields of blood kings mount to earthly thrones.

On the green slope of yonder hill they rest,
  Whose trusty swords hang in our marble hall;
But the comrade's portrait whom we love the best
  Smiles sweetly down from our own chamber wall.

THE HEART'S TENDER RECOLLECTION.

Eyes moist with emotion, cheeks wet with hot tears,
　Hearts swelling with this darkest depth of our grief, —
Attest the affection we have cherished for years
　Toward the hero whom we hailed as our valiant chief.

Oh, how heedless of that bugle's clarion voice
　Are our comrades who sleep in yonder green vale!
They regard not our victory's *éclat*, nor rejoice
　In the glamour which floats on the far-sounding gale.

THE SOLDIER'S REVERIE.

The vials of wrath are still falling to earth,
　Poured out by the demon of war;
Still strewing the field, desolation and dearth
　Show the boldest defiance of law.

On the pavement we hear the rough tramp of the steed
  And the rattle of hoofs on the plain;
The messenger comes in his ravenous greed
  To pile up the heaps of the slain.

While the sands of the hour-glass are dropping below
  And the figure of death stands above,
The sharp scythe is now mowing the swath of the foe,
  For that feels neither mercy nor love.

They fall by the sword drawn in bitterest strife,
  And some by the pestilent air,
While they march to the front with the shrill note of fife,
  And they die with no food and no care.

Oh, where is the heart that can feel others' woe,
  And in pity for man own a share,
That in sorrow and grief can some sympathy show,
  And relief to the sorrowing bear?

The beast in his lair, like the wild lion, roars
  While he tears up the flesh for his dam;
And away from his aerie the bold eagle soars
  To seize on the innocent lamb.

It is so cruel men in their butchery slay
  Each his fellow with cannon and sword;
Through the broad fields of blood they now scatter dismay,
  Where the foe lies all slaughtered and gored.

It is true that the beast dreams not he must soon die,
  But he shrinks from the strife and the pain;
While the man ever conscious where he must soon lie
  May at once find his death to be gain.

In the morn of his life his gay hopes appear bright,
  And he seeks for the pleasures in store;
In the evening his sky frowns as black as the night
  In the midst of the Newfoundland shore.

When the twilight shall kindle the height of the mountain,
  And the daybreak shall lighten the hill;
When the thirsty shall drink of the stream and the fountain
  And the draught shall disperse every ill, —

Then in paradise morning shall dawn with new splendor
  And shall dazzle his vision with light;
Then his heart shall be glad and emotions most tender,
  For the glory will ravish his sight.

*Single disconnected Stanza extracted from an Oration on
Memorial Day before a Post of the G. A. R.*

> Sleep, my dear brother, sleep,
>   Beneath this silent sod,
> Till angels sound the trump
>   Which calls thee home to God.

REMINISCENCES.

OUR LOVED AND LOST.

Blest scenes of childhood! many days and years
Have winged their angel flight through joys and tears
Since this lone wanderer forsook his home,
Through camp and field o'er this broad earth to roam.

O give me back the treasures of my love,
The hillside pasture, meadow brook and grove,
The gladsome days of youth, no more to stray
From my own New England fireside far away.

Bring back the faces of that olden time,
Long years ago at rest in holier clime;
Speak once again, my schoolmate, friend and brother;
Give me one tender kiss, my own dear mother.

Sleep thou in peace and take thy needful rest,
No cloud of grief shall reach the soul thus blest;
Bright flowers bedeck thy grave, green be the sod,
Pure be thy joy in the Eden of thy God.

Thou canst not view the stream of burning tears
Which fall like raindrops in our griefs and fears;
Thou canst not feel the pang or inward smart
Which, like a keen blade, pierceth this sad heart.

'T is not the mound which covers thee above,
Nor this cold earth that shuts thee from my love,
Nor autumn leaves upon thy bosom piled,
Nor wintry blast and storm so fierce and wild.

'T is not the stillness, nor the icy wave,
Nor yet the sleet that falls upon thy grave,
Nor drifting snows so roughly heaped on high, —
No, nor the chilly winds that whistle by.

All these I feel, but oh! how vastly more
The loneliness and gloom, the sadness sore,
Which fills my heart to the brim and overflows
My cup of sorrow with these weighty woes.

Of all these keenest woes, sad though they be,
None can so move the reins of grief in me
As one fond look upon the lonely room
Left vacant in my drear, forsaken home.

The cypress tree which shades the cheerless spot
Where lies all that is dear and ne'er forgot
Shall grow for ages, and then waste away,
Long ere my love shall wane or hopes decay.

HAUNTS TO MEMORY DEAR.

The rose which blossoms fair on Carlisle hill,
   And scatters fragrance through the dewy morn,
And sips the misty vapor from the rill,
   Hides underneath her leaf no piercing thorn.

In that dear spot my native village stands,
   Where our forefathers in the churchyard sleep;
Oft turns my heart, from home in distant lands,
   Thither to graves where Sorrow's children weep.

On that fair mound, two churchly steeples rise;
   Within those belfries, ring the calls to prayer;
Soft toll those bells, when some old neighbor dies;
   The young and aged pay due homage there.

Proud of their martial ancestors who fought,
   At Concord, Lexington, and Bunker Hill,
These sons, with monumental shafts well wrought,
   Keep green their record : 't is our Country's will.

How many a son, to grasp earth's fame, aspires,
   And craves his father's honor for his own;
Time weans no heart from love of ancient sires,
   Whose names have faded from the moss-worn stone.

Hail to brooks, woods, and hills, our childhood mates,
   Whose echoes back my wakeful memory brings;
I love those green vales where our cottage gates
   As proudly stood as castle halls of kings.

The breath of playing zephyrs, oh, how sweet!
   The murmurs of the brooklet passing by,
As notes of harp and viol softly meet
   In tuneful strains of charming melody.

Sit we awhile beneath the sylvan shade
   Of ancient elm now gnarled and warped with age,
And watch the sunbeams dancing o'er the glade,
   And glean the lessons of this mystic page.

VISION OF FUTURE SCENES.

Oh, tell me, shall yon heaven be mine at last,
  Beyond the starry host that lines the sky,
Celestial cities of the ages past,
  Where dwell inhabitants that never die?

Shall I, indeed, then wear a princely crown,
  And live in halls where saints are courtly kings,
Join that bright retinue who own renown,
  And soar to shining orbs on angel wings?

Shall I attune my harp with strings of gold,
  And hear sweet music of angelic choirs,
Live countless ages, never then grow old,
  Entranced in song and by strains of heavenly lyres

No more shall sail upon the storm-tossed sea
  My fragile bark, laden with precious store;
The wreck of ventures may return to me
  From ocean's waste of waters never more.

Green lap of earth, blue cope of sky, shall seem
    A floating spectre in the hazy light;
Fame's empty bauble, fleeting as a dream,
    Least of man's hollow toys once lured the sight.

Time was when song of nightingale was clear,
    When tree and grove and hill could all rejoice;
To woodland minstrels then I turned my ear,
    Then gladly heard the sound of Nature's voice.

Once it was sweet upon that bank to lie
    And watch the soaring eagle in his flight,
And, gazing upward, view the azure sky
    While dusky eve was fading into night.

Between two worlds there hangs a brazen door,
    Which, swinging wide upon its iron hinges,
Yields gently when the ransomed soul goes o'er,
    And on the gate of death itself impinges.

Beside the gateway two fierce dragons stay,
    Called Dread and Fear, both giants in their might,
Whose office 'tis to beckon souls away, —
    To seize and capture them while on their flight.

From here 'tis but a step to endless life,
    The starry pathway upward leads to heaven.
The bridegroom welcomes home his princely wife,
    Her escort Michael and archangels seven.

A golden string of blossoms binds her train,
    Her brow is wreathed with circlet of fair flowers,
From which drop perfumes, just as holy fane
    Bears incense on the shrine of Eden's bowers.

Didst see the stride they made from star to star,
    While, step by step, the ladder they ascended?
Or couldst thou trace their journey from afar,
    Or view their pleasure when their march was ended?

Each saint beholds strange prospects, hears new sounds;
    The wonders widen as the soul ascends;
The scenes of earth spread out to distant bounds, —
    Some of this vision pleases, some offends.

While forest, meadow, mountain still are near,
    At first familiar objects meet the view;
The landscape stretches far through countries here, —
    Above the cloudy summits all is new.

He meets companions in his airy flight;
  The twilight deepens while he floats away;
Lost in the shadows of the coming night
  Earth fades; for so the darkness ends the day.

But now the comrades of his journey speak, —
  For millions traverse o'er the self-same path,
Since heaven's the home all spirits fain would seek,
  Save those who struggle on the road to wrath.

As some belated travellers, strayed away
  Far from the road, have lost their mountain guide,
So these lone spirits, wearied through the day,
  Find to their loss that they have wandered wide;

Approach the precipice, there stand amazed,
  And tremble at the fearful chasm below,
Quaking with deadly terror, strangely dazed,
  Bewildered walk, with heavy steps and slow.

As tourists slide into the glacial cleft,
  Still tumbling down till they can fall no lower,
So sink lost souls, of every hope bereft,
  Where wrecks lie scattered on that dismal shore.

Turn hence your eyes to yonder bright blue dome,
　　Where Christian heroes mount revolving spheres;
Where noble spirits reach their blissful home
　　And dwell with God's fair angels countless years.

Now greet the ear, like roll of distant thunders,
　　Concords Divine and notes without alloy.
Saints scale the heights of heaven, where untold wonders
　　Break on their sight with pure, seraphic joy.

What power, save One Almighty, can excel
　　The strength of imp or cherub on the wing?
Or their puissant nature, who can tell,
　　As homeward they the spoils of conquest bring?

From shore to shore, between these distant spheres,
　　With lightning speed they travel in their flight;
And carry captives, with triumphant cheers,
　　To homes of joy or realms of darkest night.

If leaving heaven to visit earth below
　　Was self-denying sacrifice so great,
Then going hence to paradise we know
　　Must be the crowning gift of friendly fate.

Why murmur we that our most precious boon
  So swiftly visits us? and why complain
That our darling ones have reached the goal so soon,
  And stored their treasuries with priceless gain?

When children die, and death's dark mantles fall
  On sons and daughters thus from earth set free,
'T is sweet and blest to hear those children call,
  "Oh, weep not, mother, shed no tears for me!"

When round their bier, in sympathy and sorrow,
  Friends gather weeping, for their hearts are sore,
Look upward, muse upon that golden morrow;
  Cease from those piteous cries and weep no more.

THE CAPTURE OF YORKTOWN.

On the banks of the Brandywine Washington stood;
  His steed neighed a welcome to the morrow's affray;
While the British Cornwallis, in his petulant mood,
  Defiant, awaited the dawn of the day.

While the stars are still lighting the cool autumn sky,
  Our forces march onward to meet the stern foe;
To repair the disasters of battle, they'd try
  And confront the invaders for weal or for woe.

Through the long march of highways, our soldiers
      troop o'er,
  Till they reach the proud battlements of Yorktown's
      high towers;
They demand the surrender of the red coats' gay corps,
  And await the bold answer of these haughty powers.

These powers, more puissant than our chief can wield,
  Must disdain all his threats in their own conscious
      force;
With their disciplined troops they can master the field,
  When they fight with their strength, like the stars in
      their course.

The capture of Yorktown, by stratagem wrought,
  Would surpass the bold effort of battle, we know,
Though the skill and the wisdom of this brilliant thought
  Can secure no advantage 'gainst a vigilant foe.

While the horses are champing, their bridle bits gripped,
　And are pawing the ground with their hoofs shod with
　　　steel,
All the cavalry mounted, with sabres equipped,
　Stand there, eager to follow the trumpet's high peal.

'Midst the booming of cannon and bursting of shell,
　The infantry marching to wheel into line,
Their volleys re-echo through mountain and dell,
　While the clouds with the smoke of the battle combine.

There Washington bore his bright laurels away,
　For he nothing refused to do and to dare;
And the nations, in wonder, exultingly say
　That Yorktown with Waterloo we may compare.

As Napoleon yielded to Wellington there,
　So to Washington, now by his country adored,
While our banners were floating in mid-autumn air,
　Cornwallis reluctantly gave up his sword.

IN FAIRYLAND.

What didst thou see in fairyland?
Where goblins dwell and giants grand;
Where dwarfs and pigmies four-in-hand
Drive swiftly round with elfish band?

We saw the lofty mountain range,
The woodland delved with caverns strange,
Where fairies plan earth's marvel change,
Their locks and tresses fair arrange.

The little men and women come
And go, no bigger than your thumb;
They play the fife, and beat the drum,
And hop and skip, with busy hum.

They laugh and sing, the merry sprites,
And mimic sport of jovial wights,
And shun barbaric brawls and fights,
But frolic through the days and nights.

Accoutred fine from top to toe,
A-tripping lightly, as they go
From thorned bush to mistletoe, —
A fantasy for dazzling show.

The elfish sprites dance on the green,
As fair a sight as e'er was seen, —
As merry as the wights, I ween,
Who toss their caps for Titan's queen.

Down in the hollow of their dells,
We hear the tinkling sound of bells;
The joy of revelry it tells, —
In feast and song, the music swells.

With distant low of herded kine,
Soft notes of lute and harp combine;
Elves drain their goblets, brimmed with wine,
Pressed new and sweet from woodland vine.

The tuneful cricket joins their mirth,
Chirps for the gayety of earth;
Of echo's voices there 's no dearth,
To prove to minstrelsy her worth.

The sounds we hear, the sights we see,
Recall the lands where mortals be, —
Far less of sorrow, more of glee,
Than float the wild, tempestuous sea.

Their sky, wrought in cerulean blue,
Admits the starlight glory through, —
Just where celestial angels flew,
Sprites' busy feet their tracks pursue.

In fairyland all peace we saw, —
No bitterness of strife, no war,
No crime, which, with a lion's paw,
Makes havoc by the breach of law.

Strive, noble Man, with artful hand
To mould thy life to God's command;
While yon bright hour-glass pours the sand,
Frame this wide earth like fairyland.

TO TIME.

Stay, gentle Time, and rest thy weary wing,
While earth's fair scenes impinge their images
Upon the restless mirror of the mind.
Beneath the shade of yonder spreading elm,
Pray pause; behold the acres thou hast mown,
Harvested millions lying prostrate there;
For thou hast strewn the field with withered sheaves.
Look back upon the havoc thou hast wrought!
Thy rushing torrent carries to the main
The wreck of empires and the pride of kings,
Deep buried in the billows of the sea,
Where jutting rocks hang o'er the wasteful tide.
Old age and death, in rank and file with thee,
March to the solemn music of thy tread;
Full paces keep with thy advancing steps
And rations share e'en to the deadly breach.
Thou Cormorant! thou all-devouring Time!
Linger awhile, release thy grasp on man,
That pleasure, beauty, youth may longer stay,
As welcome guests within his gay abode.

Pause, lest we clip thy wings, and blunt the edge
Of that keen scythe which mows the nations down,
And pour the sands out of thine hour-glass bare.
Thou hast thyself grown old, as thy sere locks
And hoary beard betray thy years; thy form
So crooked and bent, thy wrinkled brow and cheek,
Tell us that cares and labors manifold,
So change thy lineaments, that even now
They know thee not, who lived when years were young.
Hear'st thou the signal voice of Him who stands—
One foot upon the land, one on the sea,
Within His hand, the keys of death and hell—
And with the tone which rings around the world
Proclaims His will, that time shall be no more?
As gaps of earthquake take down groups of men,
Eternity's abysm shall swallow thee;
Thy footprints in the sand upon the shore,
Laved by the ocean, shall be washed away;
And when this world, and all that lies within—
The birds and quadrupeds, mirrored in rocks—
Shall melt with fervent heat, and, like a scroll,
Be rolled together in the last great day,
Then shall thy reign, O Time, in terror end;
Thou shalt be hurled from thy imperial throne!

MOUNTAIN SCENES AND SOUNDS.

Step through this cleft of rock,
    Where lies the golden vein,
Nor dread the earthquake's shock,
    Nor heed the pelting rain.

The aerie-crag hangs high,
    Whereon the eagle builds;
Her nest beneath the sky
    The sunset glory gilds.

See how the lofty peaks
    In proud succession rise;
'T is there the thunder speaks,
    When lightning rends the skies.

Look where the boulder falls,
    Crashes with might and main, —
Tears through the mountain walls,
    And strikes the trembling plain.

The shepherd's bugle sounds;
  From crag to topmost hill
The thrilling note rebounds,
  The echoing valleys fill.

Fiercely the brooding storm
  Bursts o'er the clouded peaks;
Eagles, in tragic form,
  Utter wild, frantic shrieks.

The rainbow spreads an arch,
  Above this stormy scene;
Clouds tramp in leaguered march,
  Along the sloping green.

The sunlight breaking through,
  Reveals the meadows bare;
Lambs with their mother ewe
  Are feeding gladly there.

And now the storm is o'er,
  You leave the rock again,
Descend the hill once more,
  And reach the grassy plain.

THE GATE AND PATH TO LETHE.

Ah! must these hands grow cold,
  These eyes their lustre lose?
Must all these powers wax old,
  And leave no strength to choose?

Sense, taste, and sight must fail,
  The listening ear be dull;
The ruddy cheek turn pale,
  The voice to stillness lull.

The throbbing heart is faint,
  The weary pulse grows weak;
The ebbing life of saint
  Seems thus its end to seek.

The death that all men dread
  Will very soon come here;
O'er bridge of sighs, they'll tread, —
  Then go, and feel no fear.

This earth to thee is naught.
  Ah! didst thou know how soon,
Night, with deep silence fraught,
  Will swallow up thy noon?

Thou wilt not hear the wind
  That moans through yonder trees,
Nor heed the message kind
  Borne on that gentle breeze.

Beyond this vale below
  Thy sorrows will not last;
This world, with all its woe,
  Will be forever past.

Sleep on thy brow will fall,
  When shades of evening lower;
But who shall spread the pall,
  In that dark, dismal hour?

What form shall stand beside
  The couch of peaceful rest?
What voice thy soul shall guide
  To realms where saints are blest?

Lean on the trusted arm
Of some true bosom friend,
Who shields thee from all harm, —
Keeps vigil till the end.

Heed not the tears we shed,
While going on thy way;
'T was cruel when we said,
Thou must still longer stay.

The pressure of thy hand
Thrills to my inmost heart;
I hear the stern command
That bids thee now depart.

Then give us thy last word,
Uttered with feeble gasp, —
Alas! no sound is heard,
Thou canst not feel my grasp.

Those rayless orbs grow dim,
They see this light no more;
Thy soul, o'er ocean's brim,
Sets sail for heaven's bright shore.

Whispers both soft and low,
   Darkness and silence dread,
Witness to all our woe,
   Round us in anguish spread.

Missives of grief now fly
   To anxious friends most dear,
Whose sad wails rend the sky,
   While Heaven drops many a tear.

Beyond the winding-sheet,
   Beyond the bier and shroud,
The cold grave yawns to greet
   Her conquest, stern and proud.

How sad the sleep of death!
   How dark the silent tomb! —
No space for vital breath,
   No spark to light the gloom.

Within the sacred crypt,
   Beside the fathers laid,
Thy corse is well equipped
   For honors to be paid.

To death his trophy bring;
  Let pensive prayers be said;
While solemn spirits sing,
  Their requiems o'er the dead.

Alas! who now can tell,
  How tenderly they bore,
'Mid countless tears that fell,
  Thy soul to yonder shore.

Dear friend, in slumber dwell,
  Till swift-winged time flies o'er;
God's angel then shall tell
  Thy soul to sleep no more.

There rest, bereft of sense,
  Till earth remoulds thy form;
Remain through ages hence,
  Nor heed cloud, wind, nor storm.

THE MAIDEN AND THE FLOWERS.

In my garden stands a lily,
   Close beside it hangs a rose;
Near the border of the trellis,
   Many a tender tulip grows.

In my arbor sits a maiden,
   Like the flowers, she is fair, —
Gentle grace and modest beauty,
   Crowned above with nutbrown hair.

Ruby lips that breathe their sweetness,
   Honeyed dewdrops in their kiss;
Dimpled cheeks with blushing whiteness,
   Picture her unwedded bliss.

Wild flowers blossom on the hillside,
   Pouring perfumes through the breeze, —
How I love the sweet arbutus,
   Trailing by the shady trees!

Nicer, neater, my fair lady
  Fain adorns her fragrant bower,
While my heart still wastes in loving
  This bright Sibyl, my sweet flower.

When her feet, 'mid cowslips treading,
  Brush the dew, their petals bear,
Fairies, from their dreams awaking,
  Wonder at her stately air.

Knights from tournament in armor,
  Resting in her court a while,
Prize, above the gifts of princes,
  This rare pleasure, her sweet smile.

Where can beauty dwell, excelling
  Lilies that adorn her breast?
Oh, sweet fragrance of fair blossoms,
  Roses to her bosom pressed!

STORM–TOSSED.

Like a ship without an anchor, on a sea that hath no
    shore,
Sails the soul across the ocean, when the storms begin
    to pour;
And the light of yonder beacon, shrouded in its nightly
    shade,
Casts no beam upon the pathway where the dismal
    course is laid.

Hopeless onward, still a-drifting, borne along with wind
    and tide,
See her bravely, fiercely struggling, o'er the waste of
    waters wide;
While the waves are round her dashing, and her cry goes
    up in vain;
For her spars are dashed to splinters, and her sail is
    rent in twain.

Hear the bitter cry of anguish, as she rides the shoreless
    sea,
Since there's no sure power to help her, none to rescue
    can there be;
She must sink beneath the billows, overwhelmed with
    storm and wave,
And her precious cargo scattered, shall be lost, if none
    can save.

Strewn along the ocean's bottom, scattered o'er the briny
    deep,
Lies the harvest-field all shipwrecked, where the stalwart
    spirits sleep;
Buried in the gulf of waters, Jesus walks the wave-
    washed deck;
Hence, from out the grave's rough billows, Christ can
    lift the shattered wreck.

He's the wondrous, mighty Saviour, who can calm the
    angry sea,
Who can quiet all its billows, and restore lost life to thee.
Though thou traverse life's great ocean, drifting far from
    pole to pole,
Christ can soothe the troubled waters, He can cheer the
    hopeless soul.

Soul of man, how dear a treasure, in this Jesus thou
    canst find;
He hath power to still the tempest, He the raving sea
    can bind.
O'er tempestuous waves now sailing, take this Saviour
    by your side, —
O my soul! when thou art sinking, Jesus stay the
    whelming tide.

QUEST OF THE UNKNOWN BOURN.

In the wildwood on the hillside, far away from childhood's home,
Dreaming still of ancient splendor in the courtly halls
of Rome,
Lo, a pilgrim, weak and weary, fainting by the cavern's
door,
Sinks to rest, nor longer listens, heedless of the lion's
roar.

Though he climbs the lofty mountain, high upon its
crest alone,
There surveys the brilliant prospect, Cæsar on his kingly
throne ;
Charmed with visions grand in splendor, o'er the trackless earth he 'll roam,
Lost in wonder, faint and famished, yearning still for
rest and home.

O'er this earth, lone man is wandering, searching out
 some promised land, —
See him, bent and hoary, tramping with his pilgrim's
 staff in hand ;
Stranger in this foreign country, where he dreads to
 walk alone,
Native land of his forefathers, which he spurns to call
 his own.

Hero of these changing fortunes, once a bondman, now
 a king,
Mounting thrones and wielding sceptres, (crowns are toys
 that empires bring),
Slave of every menial passion, stout of heart, with iron
 nerve,
Oft he sways, but sometimes falters, born alike to rule
 or serve.

Such is man, strange contradiction, shade of demon, like
 a god ;
Vices mingled with rare virtues, make his panoply so odd.
Adam's curses he inherits, also blessings numbered seven,
Destined by ancestral birthright both for hades and for
 heaven.

Vainly struggling still for freedom, restless by divine
    decree,
Hoping, fearing, trusting, trembling, yet despondent
    though he be,
Man beholds through yonder wicket, streaming far bright
    beams of light,
On his throne a graceful figure, driving hence the gloom
    of night.

There 's the home he 's fondly seeking, there the streets
    are paved with gold ;
Hope, in visions oft revealing, shows the charms of
    wealth untold ;
Gladly there he makes his journey, lays his earthly
    mantle by,
Finds his rest, his peace and glory, in those mansions
    built on high.

THE SOUL'S VOYAGE.

On one dank evening of an autumn day,
    In sere November,
    As I remember,
I stood upon a rock, and watched the spray
    Of earth's vast ocean,
    With ceaseless motion,
Rolling in measured cadence 'gainst the base
    Of yonder cliff,
    And wondered if
The spirits dwell within that hallowed space.

Tell me, thou spirit of the untamed sea —
    By waves uprising,
    The crags baptizing —
Where all thy buried stores of treasures be?
    In vessels battered,
    O'er bottoms scattered,
Or wide outspread upon the boundless shore;
    In death's cold sleep,
    In whelming deep,
Where millions sink to rest and rise no more.

How oft the soul, like that tumultuous sea,
    With passion tossing,
    O'er barriers crossing,
Still swells and rages, from submission free;
    And, like the ocean
    In wild commotion,
Soon dashes on the rock of dark despair,
    And spends his force,
    Where ends his course,
By casting his dread burdens high in air.

See how that gallant ship sails o'er the main —
    On bounding billow,
    Her crested pillow —
Swift homeward, harboring in peace again;
    So, tempest-driven,
    With cordage riven,
The soul drifts yarely through the voyage of life —
    From perils shrinking,
    Rising and sinking —
Within the port to rest from toil and strife.

While now the crested wave leaps up on high,
    With billows whirling,
    Their summits curling,

He grasps the highest clouds beneath the sky;
  With rage still foaming,
  Through shades of gloaming,
These motions of the wave defy control;
  Where spirits hover,
  When many a brother
Casts anchor in the haven of the soul.

When first he launched upon that troubled sea,
  'Mid hopes and fears,
  With smiles and tears,
He seemed a gallant sailor, bold and free,
  Till, sailing faster
  Through grave disaster,
He reached the confines of that distant shore;
  He stood forlorn,
  By battle torn, —
No swain could count the wounds and scars he bore.

When that rough sea grows wild with wind and storm,
  The seagulls wail for
  The trembling sailor;
The howling tempest strips the vessel's form,
  Imprints the traces
  Of his embraces, —

The timid voyager seeks help in vain;
    Storms the rough air
    With vows and prayer,
Loud rings the welkin with his plaintive strain.

When the hale seaman spies the ocean's verge,
    And halts there, standing
    Near Neptune's landing,
He buffets well the strong, imperious surge,
    With lusty stroke,
    With heart of oak,
And with bold thrust, he meets the wave-washed land;
    In Heaven's kind keeping,
    O'er breakers leaping,
At last, in safety, mounts the rock-ribbed strand.

No mind can picture and no tongue can tell
    The satisfaction
    Of that transaction;
Naught else can equal, and no joy excel,
    In every nation
    Throughout creation,
The mariner's delight in reaching home;
    But who can measure
    The priceless treasure, —
The soul's abode beneath heaven's splendid dome?

ECHO.

Echo is a little brownie;
  Deep he hides in rocky caves,
Has a beard all soft and downy,
  For the rascal never shaves.

Once he watched some lovers wooing —
  He himself wooed too, I guess;
While this game he was pursuing,
  Lo! his sweetheart answered, yes.

Echo has a pretty fancy,
  And (his softness please excuse)
Calls his best girl, "sweetest Nancy,"
  Never says, "Miss Nancy Muse."

Echo now will soon be married, —
  Yes, to young Miss Muse, I think;
So his bride will then be carried,
  To her home at Stony Brink.

Fairy prophets say his quarters,
  'Neath the caverns on the hill,
Will be cheered with lovely daughters, —
  Many more are coming still.

Grace, who is this Echo's sister,
  Still a babe on cowslips fed,
Called aloud when Voco kissed her,
  Told us just the words he said.

Many a man has tried to tree her,
  While she tattled in her walk;
None of them could ever see her,
  Though they plainly heard her talk.

These same hollow woodland voices,
  When this world of life began,
Wherein nature now rejoices,
  Frightened first primeval man.

When the timid ploughboy whistles,
  Hasting through the dark alone,
Then his hair stands up like bristles,
  While his heart turns cold as stone.

Listen to his teeth that chatter!
  For he hears some frightful sound;
On the path, his footsteps clatter,
  While they tread this haunted ground.

Many footsteps coming nearer,
  From the nooks and ledges round,
All the while still growing clearer, —
  Terror fills their awful sound.

Now they seize him, — how he shivers!
  Now he utters one loud scream,
Calls for help, but none delivers;
  Wakes and finds it all a dream.

WATCHFULNESS.

Guard thou with diligence
  Passion's upheaval;
    Win thy renown.
Watch thou with vigilance,
  Lest spirits evil
    Steal thy bright crown.

Stand firm in panoply,
  Gird on thy armor,
    Unsheathe thy sword.
'Neath heaven's blue canopy
  Lurks there a charmer
    By fiends adored.

Over thy slumbering
  Angels keep vigil, —
    They never sleep.
Err'st thou in numbering
  One privilege ill,
    Good angels weep.

HYMN.

Great and eternal God,
  Source of all peaceful rest,
Take us within thine arms,
  To dwell for ever blest.

There cease we from our toil,
  From pain and sorrow rest;
Our cares and burdens fall,
  While on Thy loving breast.

Soothed by Thy comfort there,
  And there sustained and cheered,
We breathe and live in Thee,
  By Thy rich grace endeared.

Grief, fear, distress, and sighs,
  Here vex and toss the soul;
There, peace and calm repose,
  Assume their sweet control.

Brave shall our warfare be,
  Since we shall see Thy face,
Dwell in Thy smiles for aye,
  Wooed by Thy warm embrace.

(99)

CENTENNIAL HYMN OF PRAISE TO GOD.

Glad be my heart in God delighting !
  My soul with mercy He deigns to fill.
How dear His love, e'en though in smiting,
  Oft He reprove me, — I love Him still !

Goodness how great, all good excelling !
  Kindness how tender ! bounty how free !
His power so vast, all things compelling,
  Homage and worship, my God to Thee.

Anthems to God, oh, let us be singing !
  Make hymns and music His praise prolong ;
Temples and sky, your arches ringing,
  While groves and mountains echo the song.

Thanks be to God, joy to the nation !
  Angels and mortals gladly combine
Glory to give and deep adoration —
  Join ye the chorus, confess Him Divine.

Give God the praise, to Father glory !
  To Son and Spirit, whom both do send.
As 't was of old in sacred story,
  Is now and shall be world without end.

Amen.

THE DEPARTING SOUL.

The time of my departure draweth near;
Before me lie the grave, the shroud, the bier;
God hath assured my heart, I will not fear.

The word of parting must be spoken soon;
Long since I passed the brightness of the noon;
Night cometh quick, to bring my rest and boon.

Already now I see the parting tear;
Death is approaching, — he is almost here;
Joy lies beyond the tomb to bring its cheer.

Friends stand around me with their bated breath,
Questing my heart and pulse if this be death;
Nay, this is life, the answering angel saith.

What forms are these I see about my bed?
Strange figures in the air surround my head.
The hovering spirits say, "He is not dead."

They speak the truth, for now I surely live;
I change brief life for its alternative,
For Jesus Christ immortal life doth give.

DWELLING WITH CHRIST.

How peacefully man sinks to rest,
  Beneath the summer evening's shade,
So, calmly on my Saviour's breast,
  My weary head is gently laid.

There can I find the sweet repose,
  Which soothes my throbbing brain to sleep;
There gain a balm for all my woes,
  From every ill my soul to keep.

There sorrow takes its rapid flight,
  And care abashed shrinks swift away;
Corroding grief evades the sight,
  And troublous fears no longer stay.

There comfort dwells with hope and peace,
  Joy rules supreme within my heart;
There gracious gifts can never cease,
  While clinging still where none can part.

Oh, draw me nearer to Thy breast,
  Thou gracious and most loving Lord !
A place beside Thee as Thy guest,
  Within Thine arms to me accord.

There may I ever dwell secure,
  And spend my life in serving thee ;
Thus I can make my venture sure,
  In launching on the boundless sea.

The vast domain of endless years,
  Awaits my soul to set it free ;
From sorrows, griefs, and anxious fears,
  Oh take me, Lord, to dwell with thee !

THE SOUL LONGING FOR HEAVEN.

O'er the waters we shall gently glide,
   On the shore of some celestial lake;
By the bank of that sequestered stream,
   We shall rest and peaceful comfort take.

Beauty dwells upon fair Zion's hill,
   Joy and triumph sit enthronéd there;
Heaven's bright rainbow circles round the throne,
   Palaces there shine all bright and fair.

Sweetest harmonies of music swell,
   Strains melodious greet the ravished ear,
And the song my heart hath loved so well,
   In that Eden still resounds so clear.

Oh, may I that blessed rapture feel!—
   Sated pleasure in those realms of bliss;
At the feet of Jesus humbly kneel,
   From His lips receive a brother's kiss.

Bright and beautiful is yonder throng,
  Cleansed in spotless garments white and clean;
Stainless robes encircle them around,
  Fragrant roses still adorn the scene.

O'er bright cheeks, above unwrinkled brow,
  Saints and martyrs wear a golden crown;
Harps are swinging by each angel's side,
  Till at Jesus' feet they cast them down.

Pleasures brimming in their cup of joy,
  Fill their souls with overflowing streams;
Revelling in bliss without alloy,
  Saints secure their land of happy dreams.

THE SOUL'S YEARNING.

The angels with their faces thinly veiled,
  Dwell in their tents on vast Elysian fields;
The cherubim, by tempters unassailed,
  Display the splendor of their burnished shields.

Above them all sits Jesus high enthroned,
  Beside the right hand of His Father, God;
And one eternal Deity, 't is owned,
  Still rules those heavens with His benignant rod.

Soon shall we also dwell in peace and love,
  Upon the borders of that goodly land;
Soon shall our spirits join the host above,
  And share the greeting of heaven's angel band.

My longing soul looks upward to those skies;
  My zealous heart yearns for those priceless things —
Hasten, O Time! whilom thy spirit flies,
  Falter no longer on thy weary wings.

My precious Jesu! I would come to Thee;
  Help me to moult this clod of earthen clay,
Tear off this structure, leave its tenant free,
  And bear this burdened soul from earth away.

As panting hart thirsts for some clear, cool brook,
  Or wayworn traveller longs for shady grove,
So my fond spirit casts an upward look
  To Paradise, where all my fancies rove.

Weary of earth, impatient for the skies,
  Restless, we wait for God's imperious call.
On His great day, immortal we shall rise,
  And dwell for ever in His courtly hall.

The bright aurora of that cloudless day,
  Whose festive pleasures never shall be gone,
Shall find us marshalled in the host's array,
  Ever with angel armies marching on.

HOPE'S CHIME AT EASTER–TIDE.

Wake, blissful Soul, trust now thy God;
That mouldering form beneath the sod,
Clothed fresh in green, — immortal vine, —
Shall soon be thine, shall soon be thine.

Beyond the boundless ocean's roar,
Where bitter tears shall fall no more,
The anchor peacefully shall rest,
Within that port for ever blest.

No storm shall sweep across the main,
No billows rage, no wind nor rain;
No tempest swell beyond control,
To wreck the hopes of one dear soul.

That spacious dome, that princely land,
Where angels crowned in glory stand,
Fair bowers entwined with eglantine, —
Shall soon be mine, shall soon be mine.

Green meadows traced by shady rills,
Bright fields bedecked with sunny hills,
High temples towering o'er the plain,
Await this earth's immortal train.

There friends long severed gladly meet,
And taste of joys supremely sweet;
There brother's warmth and sister's love,
Share their full part with God above.

Gray templed heights, 'mid field of flowers,
Far-stretching plains with lofty towers,
Their summits wreathed with ivy vine,
Shall all be yours, shall all be mine.

For ever mine, for ever yours,
Long as eternity endures,
Those cloudless heavens and skies serene,
Shall smile above this festive scene.

When lasting ages cease to roll,
That blissful home, O yearning Soul!
Though sun and stars no longer shine,
Shall still be yours, and still be mine.

AN ELEGY ON MAUD.

Maud is my pet, Maud is my joy;
　　Kiss not her cheek too rudely now,
　　　O thou rough northwest Wind!
Did I not woo her when a boy,
　　And plight to her my youthful vow, —
　　　To her so sweet and kind?

Her sprightly step, O Lap of Earth,
　　Now toucheth thee with tender tread, —
　　　She strolls the path alone.
Treat her as child of gentle birth;
　　Thy smooth green carpet keep outspread,
　　　Nor hurt with clod or stone.

Maud is my dear, Maud is my life;
　　Guard her from breeze that bends the pines,
　　　Ye regnant Powers above!
Protect her timid soul from strife,
　　While round her form my heart entwines
　　　The tendrils of its love.

Maud is my hope, Maud is my pride ;
　Methinks I see within her eye
　　A drop which forms a tear.
There is a grief she cannot hide, —
　A breath, as if it were a sigh,
　　Is all that I can hear.

Search through the world, though we may rove,
　Where shall we find the proudest belle
　　Such grace and beauty gain ?
Save haply in their templed grove,
　Where virgins, weak with fasting, dwell,
　　Or near Ephesian fane.

Sweet flowers blossom but to fade ;
　How soon they wither and decay,
　　The roses bloom and die !
And thus the lover and the maid
　From fond embrace must part for aye ;
　　And so must Maud and I.

Upon her cheek, the maiden's blush
　Soon disappears and leaves no trace, —
　　The parching lips are still ;

The cough, the pain, the hectic flush,
  The glossy eye, the pallid face,
    All tell us Maud is ill.

With parting words, she seems to choke,
  And yet, with cheerful smiles, she greets
    The friends she loved of yore;
My name's the last she ever spoke;
  Her weary heart no longer beats,
    Her pulse can throb no more.

THE DISTRACTED MOURNER.

Yes, stand by this table the sad, vacant chair;
Fold these little garments and lay them down there;
I'll seek her, if Heaven the strength will but give;
I'll find her, — I know that she yet doth still live!

Out into the darkness the crazed mother goes,
And tells to all ghostly shades her dreadful woes.
" Did the car of Valsalva along this way drive?
I'll seek out and find her; she must be alive."

She met a bright angel in robes shining white;
She knew not that this being was only a sprite;
She spoke but with trembling in spite of her will:
" Have you seen my dear child? Is she not living still?"

"Oh, yes, thou fond mother, but one hour ago
She passed by this way, where is never a foe;
She rode in a chariot which upwards did fly, —
I know that your darling child never can die."

The mourner in wildest grief still onward flew,
To gather from strange spirits all that they knew.
" Where, where is my loved one?" she asked in dismay;
" Didst thou not behold her when she passed this way?"

" 'T is true, earthly mourner, we saw her glide by;
We watched her with rapture ascending the sky;
No more shalt thou see her on earth here below;
Through heaven's bright portals we all saw her go."

Farewell, my sweet daughter! farewell, lovely dear!
Thou hast left me on earth, no more to be here.
Christ came forth to greet thee with heart's burning love;
He holds thee enshrined in His palace above.

NAME OF JESUS.

Name of Jesus, lasting ever,
　Carve it on the granite rock;
Chisel deep to stand for ages,
　Breasting still the tempest's shock.
When the ocean rolls his billows,
　Breaking with each crested wave,
There it shines in matchless beauty,
　Shipwrecked mariners to save.

Name of Jesus, full of wonder,
　Solace of this world of woe;
Like a talisman, it teaches
　All that nations need to know.
Speaks of heaven and leads us thither;
　Shows to all the narrow way;
Offers man this free salvation,
　Triumph in the judgment day.

Name of Jesus, oh, how winning!
　Sound it in the shepherd's ear;

Listen to entrancing echoes,
    Wakened in yon caverns drear;
Tribes enchanted flock to hear it,
    Strangely held by magic sound;
Savage nations kneel to worship,
    On that consecrated ground.

Name of Jesus, oh, how precious!
    Could I soar to heights above,
There behold Him, view His splendor,
    Share His glory, taste His love;
Gladly would I there adore Him,
    Cast rich offerings at His feet,
Gold and myrrh and treasures bringing,
    Incense burning, perfumes sweet.

Name of Jesus, working wonders, —
    Lame men walk, the blind can see;
Lepers cleansed return to thank Him,
    Spotless, from disease set free.
Palsied limbs their use restoring, —
    'Twas the word that Jesus said, —
Deaf and dumb gain speech and hearing;
    Lo! His voice awakes the dead.

HEAVEN.

See sloping hills and meadows green,
Where groves and pastures crowd the scene.
Through sunlight clustered blossoms glow
And fruits in stately vineyards grow.

Fair realms of beauty, my heart sighs
To reach that home, where cloudless skies
Shall compass fields of fresh delight,
Whose splendors daze the ravished sight.

Millions, that crystal waters crave,
Come floating o'er the tidal wave;
The glittering host assembled there,
This sea of glory fain would share.

Soaring aloft to brighter spheres,
Our hopes fulfilled, and stilled our fears,
We'll reign supreme on ebon throne,
And claim the pageant all our own.

Tempestuous tossings of the mind,
The heart's forebodings left behind,
Shall cringe beneath this earth's control,
And fail to smite th' enraptured soul.

THE NUN.

The fairest lines are pencilled on her brow;
  The lineaments of beauty chiselled there;
Her face speaks marvels of her sacred vow;
  A charm supernal graces all her air.

With voice melodious, with accent clear,
  Her heart no longer dwells within her song;
Sweet music fails to pierce her listless ear;
  Her sadness tells us, she has suffered long.

Drawn by her beauty, swains from far and near,
  Cast at her feet the pledges of their love;
She spurns their offers with disdainful sneer;
  She covets only joys which wait above.

Her wedded heart withholds her treasured hand;
  Her vows in wedlock hence she never gave;
Her suitor dwells within a distant land;
  Her love lies buried in a hopeless grave.

At first a novice, then a veiled nun,
   With blighted earthly hopes her spirit riven,
She wears the marriage-ring for God's dear Son,
   Becomes the virgin bride and queen of heaven.

I LIFT MY SOUL, O GOD, TO THEE.

A HYMN.

I lift my soul, O God, to Thee,
  In earnest, sincere, humble prayer;
Within Thine arms, to shelter me,
  I cling; for none can perish there.

Great God, on Thee my hopes rely;
  My trust lies in Thy sacred Word;
O hear the needy suppliant cry,
  While by Thy grace, my heart is stirred.

Thy gracious and benignant smile
  Can cheer the saddest mourner's heart, —
Come Thou and dwell with me a while,
  And from my bosom ne'er depart.

Thou sendest comfort and sweet peace,
  In every sorrow, pain and grief;
Thou causest all our woes to cease,
  And givest to all fears relief.

Thou turnest sorrow into joy,
   And changest sadness into bliss;
In all Thy gifts there's no alloy;
   After Thy blow, we feel Thy kiss.

Upon Thy bosom I feel calm;
   Upon Thine arm I lean content,
Still safe from every fear of harm;
   So shall my heavenly life be spent.

ON THE STORMY SEA.

Help him, O gracious God, that sailor lad,
Tossed by tempestuous winds upon the sea;
Lashed to the giddy mast, and wet with brine,
Against him dashed by yonder rolling tide.
Bold, brave and fearless, clings he to the yard,
Amidst the wanton vaultings of the waves.
See how the curling crests leap to the clouds;
Their spray bedews the seaman's cheek with tears,
Drenches his jacket and tarpaulin garb, —
First dipped in billows, then tossed up on high
Even to the summit of the angry sky.
The prayer of penitence upon his lips,
Reaches to highest Heaven, that hears his plea.
Behold his mother's constancy, who waits
In her lone cottage, on the shore, at night,
And sets the lighted candle near the pane,
To guide her lost boy homeward through the storm.
Her agitated bosom swells and heaves,
Like the ever restless tide which wildly beats, —
A throbbing pulse against the rocky shore.

Equally sweet in tenderness of love,
The Father, sitting on His throne above,
Or standing on the threshold of His home
Beyond the stars, looks through the latticed door,
Still watching for the sparrow as she falls,
Sees that lone lad and hears his bitter cry;
And as the Master once by His command,
Stilled the rough Tiberian waves of Galilee,
So that same Lord now holds within His grasp,
The lightning's lurid flash, and quells the storm,
And soothes the waters into peaceful calm.
God's pity wrests one from the yawning gulf,
While round the sea a hundred wrecks lie strewn;
Millions lament the tragic fate of sons,
Husbands, and brothers in that charnel house,
Where bones lie bleaching on the ocean's bed.
When Captain Worden, with his gallant crew,
Sailed by the cape of stormy Hatteras,
His staunch ship foundered in the furrowed deep;
Seamen and gunners sank beneath the flood.
The wrecks, which furnish food for hungry sharks,
Splash through the waves, whose waters close above,
Nor show one single breach to mark their graves.
Like seagulls, ever restless on the wing,

Above the chasm, draped in a wreath of cloud,
Their spirits hover close around their graves;
No eye of mortal, till the veil is rent,
Can penetrate that mystic world of shades,
Or recognize with skill those ghostly forms.
Who shall explore the paths of that vast deep,
Where those torn halyards lie beside the keel
Of ships wrecked on the shoals or ragged rocks,
Whelmed by the storm upon the raging sea?
Or who can count the myriad skeletons
Of men strewn by the tempest on the shore?
The great Armada, pride of Spanish fleets,
Once ploughed the main near Britain's sea-girt isle,
But, driven by adverse winds on hostile shores,
Blindly embraced her melancholy fate,
Vanquished in ocean by the God of storms.
The night is dark, the wild winds fiercely blow,
While on the deck the captain shouts command;
Shrill through the cordage screams the albatross,
The warship stranded lies upon the beach,
Disorder and confusion reign supreme;
Crash goes the timber with the creaking mast!
She springs a leak, the waters rush within,
The fated crew, lost in the hungry sea,

Some sink, some swim, some to the lifeboat cling,
While others struggle on the broken wreck;
Now mariners lie pillowed on the sand.
Oh, thou most treacherous and inconstant sea,
Emblem of earth's vicissitudes and cares,
O'er which the ship of human life now sails,
Amidst the tempest on the rocky shoals,
Toward that fair haven where the soul finds rest.
Shield thou my bark from those rough winds of heaven,
Which smite her spars, and beat against her prow!
Ye spirits from the vast, majestic deep,
Which swarm around and hover in mid-air,
Control my skiff upon the pathless waves;
And, when these billows threaten to engulf her,
Take ye the compass, seize the giddy helm,
Subdue proud tempests, tameless in their rage,
Find port to anchor in my own dear land.

THE METAMORPHOSIS.

Hurt not the worm, nor kill him with thy tread,
For he is high-born as thyself; from earth
And dust ye both had lowly origin.
Oh! pity that poor creature, weakest of all,
Which crawls upon the ground, defenceless, dumb.
Though sees he not, yet feels he thy rude touch;
Deal gently, kindly, with thy brother twin.
Thou wast thyself a worm until evolved
By ages, which transformed thee to thyself,
At present higher in life's scale of being;
So will his offspring reach a pinnacle
Lofty as thine.   Though truly thou may'st boast
Of lineage from kings, humility
Sits on thy brow, indeed, with fairer grace
Than doth thy crown.

Crush not the cocoon in his fragile shell;
The spark of hidden life lies there encased.
Mute sleeps the form; nor tells his agony,
When bruised with heedless step that life expires,

As dies the candle's flame puffed by the wind.
Who knows what ghostly apparition flies
From those strait confines of an earthly mold?
Death comes not; hear the crackling cords which bind
Imprisoned life within that frail abode,
Where dwells the chrysalis in beauty's guise,
So gorgeously bedecked with gems and pearls.
Didst see the bud unfold her purple leaves?
So doth the cocoon burst his brittle cell,
Rises on wings of joy to soar aloft,
And heavenward flies to reach his distant home.

TO VESTA.

List to that music which floats in mid-air, —
Hear'st thou not, Vesta, so lovely and fair?
The tones are so sweet that they charm every sense —
List, Vesta, enchanted, and move thou not hence.

Gaze on the rose, so beautiful, so neat;
Sniff up its odor, so fragrant, so sweet;
Snatch off some rose blossoms, so pretty and fair;
Weave buds with tresses of thy raven hair.

Look on this pearl, now so clear and so white;
Mark how it gleams in the beams of the light;
Beauteous and costly, we'll store it with care —
How precious and priceless! how goodly and fair!

Here lie a ruby, an emerald, a gem,
Crown of rich lustre, bright diadem;
A diamond here with glistening sheen, —
All clustered together may haply be seen.

These do I give thee, fair Maiden, be mine;
All these for thy hand shall ever be thine.
Trust me, dear Vesta, and grant me thy love;
The world and its treasures, I prize thee above.

Sweeter than roses, and whiter than pearls,
Thy lips and thy brow are entwinéd with curls;
Thine eyes are more sparkling than diamonds bright, —
Have pity, dear Maiden, on this hapless wight.

No music so sweet as thy charming voice, —
O give me thy heart, and bid me rejoice!
No perfume so fragrant as thy gentle breath, —
O grant me thy love, and rescue from death!

Canst thou say nay, and thus drive me to madness?
Thus bury my life in dark gloom and sadness?
Dost thou speak that word which pierces with dread,
Like keen shafts of lightning, striking me dead?

O grant me thy presence! I ask for nought more.
O speak the word aye, and all will be o'er!
A thrill of sweet ecstacy, my soul shall employ;
My light heart shall dance with emotions of joy.

AN ODE TO THE SUN.

O thou bright Sun! lovely art thou and fair;
    'T is thou alone that see'st always day;
Thy daughters hast thou scattered everywhere,
    To chase the darkness of the night away.

Wouldst thou not choose one moment's precious gloom;
    Exchange thy beams for darkness; drive afar
The tediousness of light, and in its room,
    Welcome transforming to some rayless star?

How many worlds, 't is thine to gaze upon;
    Thou seest only noblest deeds of men, —
The brightest hemisphere of earth and moon;
    But darkest crimes are hidden from thy ken.

Thou art the type of that great moral Sun
    Whose beams of righteousness illume our earth;
Before creation's dawn, He had begun
    To blaze, a meteor of celestial birth.

When time shall cease, O Sun, thy light must fade;
  His beams shall shine with brilliant lustre still;
With eyes undimmed, and clouded with no shade,
  We shall behold Him on God's holy hill.

Grant me, O Sun of righteousness divine!
  To share the splendor of Thy noontide ray;
Dawn on my heart; within my spirit shine;
  Transform my darkness into cloudless day.

ODE TO THE OCEAN.

Roll on, wild ocean, thy tumultuous tide
  Marks night and day, with mighty ebb and flow
As on thy bosom, earth's vast navies ride,
  So o'er thy waves, man's richest treasures go.

The boundless ages, mirrored in thy flood,
  Dash rudely 'gainst the rocky shores of time;
And as thy waters have been stained with blood,
  So future years and past trace human crime.

That Power which doth eternity command
  Restrains thy fury by His firm control;
Holds thee, as well, within His hollow hand,
  Or bids thy mighty billows onward roll.

What sage can count the drops within the main,
  Or tell the grains upon thy shore's dry sod, —
Thy lowest depths can fathom, or can drain,
  Or sound the deep, dark mysteries of God?

The seas are many, but the earth is one, —
  A proper emblem of the triune God.
All oceans blending through earth's channels run,
  Extend their compass, spreading far abroad.

How many millions hast thou swallowed down
  Within thy hungry jaws, insatiate still?
How many bones of men of great renown,
  There mouldering lie, and thy dark caverns fill?

Now thou art hungry, crying still for more;
  Thy swelling tides devour the good and brave,
Wrecked on thy waves, or dashed against the shore, —
  No ear could hear their cry, no power could save.

Wrought into fury by tempestuous winds,
  Thy heartless waves against proud vessels dash;
At such a moment, when the storm begins,
  Bold seamen tremble in the lightning's flash.

Three great ones, — ocean, God, eternity:
  The first exists but mostly to devour;
The second shows divine paternity;
  The third continues, as an endless hour.

OUR CHIEFTAIN.

Vincit omnia potestas Dei.

There is no grand, sublime, or lofty verse,
Which aims our hero's merit to rehearse,
Or travailing to compass fame so great,
Can reach the measure of his princely state.

Grant stood on earth, like some majestic elm,
Whose towering summit bends to overwhelm,
As when the woodman's axe cuts through the core,
It crashing falls, destroying all before.

He stood; and fell by death's relentless blow,
Laid down his sword to one all-conquering foe;
But when he fell, he crushed all hearts before,
And naught below can his great worth restore.

That he was brave, no soldier can deny;
Ask, "Was he great?" the whole world answers, "Aye."
Magnanimous was he, as we are told;
He would not sell integrity for gold.

When victory perched on his banner proud,
The nation for revenge still called aloud;
He sheathed his sword, commanded war to cease;
Quoth he to rebel chiefs, "Let us have peace."

How many nights upon the mountain side,
Encompassed by the darkness, did he ride
Through storm and tempest, as he watched with care
The hardships of the soldier he must share.

He scans the car of Phœbus, god of day,
All red with blood and gore to man's dismay;
That sun shall set before the battle's done;
The moon shall wane, ere yet the field is won.

Upon the distant plain, the gallant foe
Have pitched their tents in line, a martial row;
Our chieftain plans his next day's battle there,
And moves his column on with dext'rous care.

He meets a gallant, brave, heroic foe,
Claimed justly as his peer by all who know,
Equal in fame, the mighty chieftain Lee,
Who could defy all powers on land or sea.

As bold Achilles fought with Hector brave,
So Grant with Lee; the Union he must save.
No fraud can capture Richmond with decoy,
As troops in wooden horse once entered Troy.

The pagan his brave father deifies,
No less should we our Christian hero prize.
If all the nations honor Robert Lee,
No less in fame his conqueror must be.

The Southern chieftain all mankind admire.
What soldier equal honor can acquire?
None but the hero who can him defeat,
And, vanquishing, can compass his retreat.

The Southern hero let all people praise,
And mausoleums to his glory raise;
Then grander monuments shall Grant endow,
Chaplets of laurel shall adorn his brow.

The North and South, well poised in warlike power,
Behold the scale descend in Fortune's hour,
For Fate's decree stands not in human might,
'T is God awards the victory to right.

DIRGE O'ER OUR CHIEF.

Since Grant is gone, my harp is all unstrung,
Nor can I lift my voice, nor tune my tongue,
Lest they express my grief with doleful sound,
As when we first stood on his sacred mound.

Touch lightly, gentle Bard, those tender strings,
Sad memories to my soul their music brings;
Too soon death came to lay our chieftain low, —
My heart was shattered by that cruel blow.

Our chief was great in thought, as in his fame;
Large also in his heart, as high in aim :
The nation has been weeping since he died,
And comrades worship him now deified.

His sad departure plunged this land in woe;
Her sons curse death, as man's relentless foe,
But high Olympus, stored with grateful joy,
Bestows its welcome, where no griefs annoy.

The angels haste to crown our noble chief;
They bow in worship, while we bend in grief:
For him they chant their songs on thrones above,
And station him supreme, through Jesus' love.

REQUIEM FOR ABSENT COMRADES.

Can solemn lyrics reach the lofty theme,
Or sages tell to comrades our esteem?
With drooping wing strength fails the muses nine,
Nor can our verse ascend to heights divine.

On one bright morn the sun arose in blood;
Through that sad day he shone o'er field and flood.
Chiefs saw battalions marshalled at their call,
Whole armies routed, and brave columns fall.

When day is ended and the battle done,
The sword is sheathed, the victory is won;
Far from that bloody field their footsteps roam,
They cease their weary march, arrive at home.

Our comrades rest on that far distant shore,
Where now to arms the drum-beat calls no more.
They sleep; the ear is deaf, the voice is still;
It wakes them not, the trumpet loud and shrill.

The host is marshalled on Elysian plains,
No more to hear the bugle's warlike strains,
No longer to fill up those serried ranks,
But called to stack their arms on Eden's banks.

Their mortal forms, enclosed in lonely graves,
Or buried deep beneath the ocean waves,
Which ever rest, in silent darkness still,
Can hear no reveillé, and feel no ill.

They left us shadowed in the deepest woe,
Hearts rent with anguish by that sorrow's blow;
We mourn their loss, nor can our sadness cease,
Until some kindly grave shall grant us peace.

Farewell, dear Comrades! many call you brothers, —
As father, son, or husband mourned by others;
In those green pastures, where ye calmly dwell
By fountain, stream, or hillside, fare ye well.

OUR BROTHER SLEEPS.

Our comrade challenged Nature's tooth unkind,
  When forth he launched o'er boundless seas to roam;
He left this cottage drenched in tears behind,
  Transformed to cloudy, dark, and wintry home.

With lispings sweet as tiny infant's breath
  He witches darkness from his couch away.
He wreathes his lips, he smiles at gloomy death,
  And silently awaits heaven's dawning day.

He peaceful sleeps beneath the placid dome;
  No fleecy cloud obscures the bright blue sky;
He rests within the chamber of his home;
  His soul trips fleeting through the halls on high.

Heaven's judgments must all creatures fain revere,
  Fixed in decree by righteous powers above;
The sting of disappointment feels severe,
  Bitter as crossings in affairs of love.

Rest, my dear brother, on thy pallet sleeping,
   Sweet be thy dreams beneath this earthly clod;
Sleep till the angels, gathered round thee weeping,
   Shall sound the trump which calls thee home to God.

Peace dwell within the borders of thy tent,
   Whose curtains shut out every grief and sorrow.
Stay in thy bivouac; when the night is spent,
   The sun shall rise upon the golden morrow.

NATURE IN PANORAMA.

THE CREATOR'S PRAISE.

How noble and sublime the thought that all
The compass of the world, the vast abyss,
The hosts of heaven, the mighty universe,
With all the countless thronging habitants,
And every atom of the depths profound,
The living creature, beast, bird, angel, man,
Stars, planets, suns, are but the breath of Him
Who spake the word and they came forth from naught.
Let heaven and earth then worship at His shrine.
The wren which chirps so sweetly on that bough,
The rill that murmurs o'er its stony bed,
The wind which whistles through those forest trees,
The humming insect and the buzzing bee,
Are singing anthems to their Maker God.
Shall man alone refuse to hymn his praise?
The works of nature how sublime they are!
The golden light, the balmy atmosphere,
The river, forest, ocean, rugged heights,

Deep cataracts and waterfalls, dark caves
And subterranean passages, the heaven's
Blue dome above us, and the starlit sky,
All deftly joined in one majestic world,
Impress us with the grandeur of their form
And kindle admiration for their being.
Let man pay reverence and honor then
To their Creator, proudly prized his own.

NATURE'S EVOLUTION AND TEACHING.

It recks not which philosophy prevails,
Within the protoplasm were potent germs
Which erst developed every form of life ;
And He who made at first the bioplasm
Created then all crude varieties
In embryonic state, and gave each power
To bridge the chasm of every missing link,
To spring across the gap of species lost.
Nor is Omnipotence the less renowned
For making all things by one single word,
Than by the fiat oft repeated o'er.
All nature moves within the hollow hand
Of Him who guides the ocean, stars, and spheres
Through endless space, along their trackless course,

And, with imperial sceptre, calmly sways
Rebellious nations in their angry strife.
Ye Forms of Beauty, stamped in nature's mold,
Impress your mystic pages on the brain,
Where memory may grasp their theme at will.
Ye Powers of Air, that write mysterious lines
Upon the forest leaves, or scattered ferns,
Along the wilds of deserts, help us read
Those truths, which the Great Teacher bids us know.
Ye unseen Spirits, Powers invisible,
Surrounding these vast planetary spheres
Crowding the crevices of spacious realms,
Display your sovereign sway through nature's works.

THE SPECTACULAR SCENE.

O Nature! fair as Eden's lovely bowers,
Thy hillsides, blooming with the flowers of spring;
Decked in arbutus, spread their smiling glades
To greet the sweet embraces of the sun;
The king of day, unwearied in his course,
Has reached the top of his aerial dome.
There paused an instant, seated on his throne,
While from his sparkling diamond crown of light,
He scatters beams to regions most remote.

The farthest corners of the universe,
Beyond the distant suns and radiant stars,
Intensifying fully their rich splendor,
With intermingled rays of kindred light.
On his swift chariot-wheels, he now descends
The western slope of that vast hill whose base,
Washed by the tides of ocean, skirts the brink
Of our horizon on its outer edge, when lo!
While yet his face, wreathed in encircling smiles,
Looks earthward, there he first beholds, far down
Below the ethereal sky, contending winds,
Engaged in earnest fight for mastery;
Weeping their misty vapors, till they form
Majestic clouds, whose fierce artilleries
Clash in the vault of heaven in deadly strife.
From cloud to cloud, shoots forth the lightning sharp,
Resounding thunder, rumbling o'er the earth,
Wakes the loud echoes from the rocks and hills.
Terrific scenes of majesty and horror,
Drive children screaming to their mother's arms,
Where they may find sure shelter from all harm.
Tall and majestic pines and leafy oaks,
Cast their deep shade across the peaceful glen,
Where foliage in luxuriant verdure waves;
Primeval forests, swaying in the storms

Of centuries, still rear their lofty heads,
Above the mountain-tops, unto the skies.
Earth holds deep caves, ribbed with the creviced rock,
Where wild beasts, sheltered from the hunter's fire,
Conceal their cubs, in safe seclusion reared.
Within those jungles of the forest wild,
On Himalaya ranges, lions roar
For prey to feed the maws of hungry whelps.
As when gigantic oaks, beneath the stroke
Of some strong woodman's axe, topple and fall
With heavy crash to earth, the startled deer
Bounds through the thicket with his utmost speed;
So, when the roaring of the beast affrights
The timid mountain goat, like some weak hare,
He springs for life away o'er rugged hills,
And rests not till he reaches his safe fold.
Within the clutches of a tiger's grip,
Defenceless lambs must struggle all in vain.
When stags have brushed the velvet from their horns,
Elks dropped their antlers near some bubbling spring;
With strength augmented, vital powers renewed,
So can they gallop through the copse like wind.
When crawls the serpent from his slimy skin,
With deadly poison in his fangs, he grasps
The cozened victim in his tightened coils,

And, gorged with blood, impales the dying wretch.
Moulting his plumes, the eagle soars on high;
With bolder flight he mounts above the clouds.
His steady gaze, fixed on the sun, reveals
The brightness of his piercing eye; he swoops
And seizes in his talons that stray lamb;
He proudly seeks his aerie, where he feeds
His young with dainty morsels of his prey.
The white-winged ship, how like a bird she flies
Across the pathless depths of wasteful sea!
Bending her mast beneath the fierce, wild wind,
She rolls and tosses on the crested waves.
Like Wisdom's ancient statue, sits enthroned,
Upon Olympian top of Alpine's peak,
The goddess Reason, while beneath her feet
Dwell everlasting snows and glacial stream,
With cracks and crevices, which onward move,
Down to the peaceful vale which sleeps below.
O'er Mont Blanc's head, with blustering whirlwind
    crowned,
The bleak, cold Arctic pours a wintry blast;
Wild Boreas blows, his breath in fury spent,
Tornadoes rage and revel in their power. —
The curtain falls on panoramic scenes;
Turn off the light, go forth, view Nature's self.

GRANT'S LAST BATTLE.

The falchion of our warrior knight,
　Swings loosely by his belted side.
And crested for the bloody fight,
　He mounts his steed with courtly pride.

On, on, he speeds, nor checks her course,
　He gallops to the gory plain ;
He halts beside his marshalled force, —
　Surveys the host of soldiers slain.

The field, with blood and carnage red,
　Lies strewn where mortal heroes fell.
The braves, that for their country bled,
　Feel leaden missiles, shot and shell.

'Mid smoke of battles armies sway,
　By quick advance and swift retreat;
While each in turn disputes the day,
　Nor owns as yet a sure defeat.

The contest waxes fierce and strong;
  The nation's fate in peril stands;
Poised in the scale, where rights belong,
  Hang trembling hopes of mighty lands.

The surly cannon's horrid roar,
  The sharp, shrill peal of musket's sound,
The clarion note of bugle corps,
  The tramp of hoofs on battle ground, —

All these our fearful spirits stir,
  And shake our souls with awful dread;
Thrust in our hearts the keenest spur,
  Thrill through us o'er the ghastly dead.

The messengers, in hottest haste,
  Swift skim the field on chargers fleet;
They shout across the savage waste:
  "The victory is now complete!"

.   .   .   .

In honor's course years speed away,
  The evening shadows darkly fall;
Pale on his couch the chieftain lay,
  And tears bedewed McGregor's hall.

We saw the train move slowly on,
  While weeping throngs in silence passed;
Heard this refrain, when Grant was gone : —
  "Life's grandest battle's o'er at last!"

THE CRUISER BROOKLYN.

Look how the cruiser leaps the dock,
    When launched upon the briny wave!
While ocean trembles with the shock,
    And her first plunge proves her most brave.

Sail on, dear ship, o'er earth's broad sea,
    And carry hence across the main
The precious ventures prized by me,
    And bring them safely home again.

Let no rude billows wreck the craft;
    Let no wild storm create alarm;
But gentle winds shall softly waft
    This goodly vessel free from harm.

Down deep in ocean's rocky bed,
    Lie skeletons of shipwrecked men,
Who sleep among the peaceful dead,
    Till summoned forth to life again.

Ten thousand souls, throughout these years,
　　Pay tribute to the hungry waves ;
And widows mourn, with patient tears,
　　Far distant from those silent graves.

When fiercest battle tests the day,
　　When by his gun stands each brave man,
Then all the world shall proudly say,
　　The cruiser Brooklyn leads the van.

In hottest fight, on· hostile seas,
　　With Cuban warships ruled by Spain,
Her strength and valor shall with ease
　　Cause us the victory to gain.

No armored gunboat shall defend,
　　Which ploughs the main with iron keel;
No proud armada may contend,
　　Though panoplied with guns of steel.

She stands like adamantine wall,
　　Protects the fleet from volleys dire ;
Where shot and shell now thickest fall,
　　She stands against the broadside fire.

Now see the staunch, majestic form;
   She sniffs the breeze with flag unfurled,
And bold to ride through fiercest storm,
   She skims the sea, a model world.

See how she rides the deep blue sea!
   In beauteous pride she floats along;
A fairy queen she seems to be, —
   So trim, so beautiful, and strong.

Above the caverns of the deep,
   The trackless waste that wrecks lie on,
Where myriads of seamen sleep,
   Bird of the sea, fly on! fly on!

Through calm and tempest, wind and storm,
   By maelstrom near Norwegian shore,
By fell Charybdis' rocky form,
   Where wildest waves and torrents roar,

Fly swift away from Siren's coast;
   Beware her craft of deadly wrong:
Whene'er the mermaid charms thee most,
   Fly from her sweet, beguiling song.

Ride deftly o'er the crested wave,
  Till danger's hostile threats shall cease,
Where fleets and navies, strong to save,
  Cast anchor in eternal peace.

.   .   .   .

Oh, how she rides o'er the blue, rolling ocean,
  Swiftly out-racing her rival's high score!
Now watch her proud form, her tremulous motion,
  'Mid the cheers of admirers, she reaches the shore.

THE BRIGHT HEREAFTER.

The time will come when all these toils shall cease;
   Our future home will then be free from tears.
Land of triumphant song and holy peace,
   Enduring firm through everlasting years.

No burden, grief, or pain shall last for aye;
   In heaven no cloud shall lower, no storm shall fall;
No night be there, but bright and glorious day;
   Long severed friends shall answer to our call.

On earth our hopes may fail, comrades may die,
   And all our brightest prospects frustrate end;
But disappointments reach not past the sky,
   Where fond content and satisfaction blend.

In heaven will be no war, no sword, no grave,
   For nations all in amity agree;
There'll be no tempest on the ocean's wave,
   No shipwrecks there upon a wind-swept sea.

(157)

'Tis one majestic temple whose clear sky
  Is canopied above with heaven's blue dome;
Arched like the vault of Staffa pillared high,
  Now yearns my soul to reach that blissful home.

Hope pointing upward, like prophetic seer,
  Foretells what joy and glad delight shall fill.
Ecstatic rapture, bliss supreme, shall cheer
  This spirit when the weary heart lies still.

TRIUMPHAL MARCH OF FREEDOM.

Proud conqueror, borne on mighty eagle's wings
   O'er cloud-capped mountain tops, we gladly see.
Through stately halls and palaces of kings
   Our hero speeds to set the nations free.

Her onward course, with spear and pointed lance,
   Shall cross the ramparts of yon castle wall;
While on her way, beneath·her fiery glance,
   The trembling hosts of tyranny shall fall.

No greaves, nor helmet strong, nor coat of mail
   Protects her form, invulnerable to steel;
She bares her breast to every stormy gale,
   And rides on, godlike, — swift as chariot wheel.

The cruel bastion totters in her track;
   She strikes down thrones and thrusts beneath the
     flood
Machines of torture, guillotine, and rack,
   And Pompey's pillar runs with Cæsar's blood.

Let Freedom live, for by her magic wand
   She strikes the shackles from each gloomy slave;
Till nations vie to honor her command;
   O'er people of all lands her banners wave.

FROM THE TEMPEST TO THE HAVEN.

Shipwrecks lie scattered on the ocean wide;
  Wild roll the billows on the pathless shore,
Lifting their cargoes o'er the mountain tide,
  Frighting the nations with their constant roar.

Terror now sways o'er this realm far and wide;
  Storm-kings are holding their violent reign;
Torrents are rushing down yon mountain's side,
  Spreading rough havoc through village and plain.

Flames are consuming our cities and towns;
  Death is destroying the young and the old;
Pain, sadness, or grief with all men abounds;
  Half our deep misery can never be told.

Church bells, resounding in sweet, solemn chime,
  Tell us how soon shall earth's troubles cease;
Silently onward move the wheels of time,
  Bearing their burdens toward the gates of peace.

Soon shall we mount up to that shoreless sea
  Where the waves seek rest in one endless calm;
We will dwell in the shade of a vast banyan tree,
  By the gardens of olives in the land of the palm.

Soar we on high borne by sable, fleet wings;
  We will rest by the banks of some shady rill;
We will drink from the cool fount, as it springs
  In sparkling waters from out the green hill.

BY CRYSTAL FOUNTAINS.

By crystal fountains and clear, purling streams,
   Down in the meadows where sweet lilies bloom;
Thy soft hand folded in mine, as if in dreams,
   Lead me, love, cheerily far from all gloom.

Daisies and daffodils and sweet-scented roses
   Breathe their mild perfumes on midsummer air;
And bright golden buttercups, queen of wild posies,
   Shed their sweet fragrance, while we linger there.

The tall, stately elm and wide-spreading oak
   Cast cooling shadows o'er the green, velvet lawn,
Where, seated in silence, with thoughts never spoke,
   We listen to wild nature's voices at dawn.

The murmuring of brooklets, the singing of birds,
   Blending in harmony with their clear, vocal air,
Charm all our senses with their "song without words,"
   While we gaze upon scenery most lovely and fair.

YOUTH'S DESTINY.

Oh, couldst thou know, vain youth, how soon
　　The bloom upon thy cheek will fade,
　　　　As summer flowers decay!
The morn of life will change to noon,
　　Then sink to rest in evening shade
　　　　And quickly speed away.

Thy life with hope may yet be crowned,
　　Thy thorny path with roses strewn
　　　　May lead to wondrous joy,
Where fields of pleasure may be found,
　　Where thorns and briers were never known
　　　　And bliss hath no alloy.

Beyond the rage of stormy seas,
　　Above this earth's most fretful skies,
　　　　Where gloomy darkness lowers,
Spread glades and vales and verdant leas;
　　And there the park of Eden lies
　　　　Compact with shady bowers.

Soon cares begin to knit thy brow,
   And furrow wrinkles on thy cheek;
     Thy hoary locks grow bare.
The fatherland draws nearer now, —
   The home that earthly pilgrims seek
     Awaits thee beckoning there.

When bends thy form with weight of years,
   Thy shoulders stoop, grow stiff with age,
     With tottering steps do fall,
New youth and beauty banish fears,
   Fresh tasks thy heavenly powers engage,
     Swift angels serve thy call.

THE BROOK.

Glide on, bright stream, thou hast no care;
   In sportive glee, still e'er go on:
Through pastures green and meadows fair,
   With childish playfulness, flow on.

Here wide and deep, with waters slow,
   Where lily blossoms crowd the space,—
How silent is thy gentle flow,
   While rushes bend to kiss thy face!

There whirling eddies toss the leaf,
   Which from its twig is rudely torn,—
Wrecked on thy bosom's savage reef,
   By dancing ripples, wildly borne.

See children sporting on thy brink,
   Where boys delight to bathe and swim;
The lowing kine come down to drink,
   And sip their nectar from thy brim.

The startled hind, at close of day,
  Pricks up her ears and bounds along,
Till, near thy waters, held at bay,
  She dreads the hunter's clarion song.

Roll on, thou tributary tide,
  Pay thy vast debt to yonder river;
Flush with thy flood his swollen side,
  Yield tribute to the mighty Giver.

Sweet Concord, fairest of the plain!
  Deep in thy stream thy jewels lie;
As o'er thy breast each throbbing vein
  Mirrors the image of the sky.

Thy current hastes with giant tread,
  Eagerly on its rocks among;
Short wavelets dance on stony bed,
  Whose music blends with thrush's song.

. . . .

FINALE.

Flow on, doughty stream, far away from thy fountain,
  Chafe thy banks still onward with trembling emotion;
Pursue thy fleet course by village and mountain, —
  Flow on, like man's life, to eternity's ocean.

NOCTURNAL RECREATIONS.

When the stars are brightly shining,
   'T is the time for clever thought;
Round the woodbine, gently twining,
   Wreathe the deeds that man hath wrought.

Carve upon the sculptured marble,
   Picture on the painted leaf,
Scenes that pen may choose to garble, —
   Stories piquant, blithe, and brief.

Sing some mirthful song or ditty;
   Tell the tale of knightly swain,
Who, in country, town or city,
   Loved and lost and loved again.

Tread the Terpsichoric measure,
   Fill the cup with brimming cheer;
Spend the night in gladsome pleasure,
   Till the dawning lights appear;

Or, if heart grows weak and weary,
　And the eyelids droop and close,
Sink to rest in darkness dreary, —
　Find thy pillow's sweet repose.

Then shall morning greet thee waking, —
　Soul refreshed and spirit cheered;
From thy dreamy slumbers breaking,
　Thou shalt haste to scenes endeared.

ODE TO LIBERTY.

Behold the brave form of sweet Liberty now!
   O Liberty, stand till the tempest drives o'er!
Since murderous hands have been laid on thy brow,
   Man pities thee, bleeding, with foes at thy door.

On, on to the triumph, with victory's crown!
   We hail the proud chieftain that shelters our land;
Thy courage in battle hath won thee renown;
   Lead on thy bold warriors, thy valiant command.

Since demagogues throttled thee, national pest,
   And tyrants have trampled, enthroning their kings,
And so many arrows are hurled at thy breast,
   Thou mountest above them on silvery wings.

Live on, thou immortal, exalted in worth,
   And ages eternal shall dig thee no grave;
Thy chariot wheels dash through the courts of the
      earth:
   Ride onward, till no land possesseth a slave.

MELANCHOLY BODINGS.

Oh! the gushing of sorrow from the tides of emotion
  When the friends that we love are no more,
Like the break of the billow from the wide, rolling ocean
  When he dashes his waves on the shore.

We may bend like the willow when the heart melts
    with anguish,
  And thus silently grieving we weep still,
While the swains sadly droop and the maids darkly
    languish
  In the hall by the tower on the hill.

See the cloud! oh, how black, and the night wind so
    chilly!
  The lone pilgrim in darkness delays,
As he stumbles o'er paths through the way rough and
    hilly,
  Where the heartbroken wanderer strays.

When the soul finds no respite in hospice or tavern,
  And the spirit sinks grave and demure,
Then we groan stoutly chambered in wild, wanton
    cavern,
  Where the sorrows of life dwell secure.

There the palaces built and the grand, rocky castles
  Shall enclose the dread forms of dismay,
While the pains and the griefs and the groans with
    their vassals
  Shall form armies in hostile array.

When the griefs thus imprisoned shall burst from
    their trammels,
  As impelled by their fury so strong,
They shall mount up on pinions with golden enamels,
  And shall smite heaven's gates with their song.

Wilt Thou rescue and help, O Thou great God of pity!
  Thy poor people and children distressed?
Send to earth some relief from that beautiful city,
  Where the weary and laden get rest.

THE PLEASURES OF CHILDHOOD.

No other spot of earth's so sweet,
  Through all the world though we may roam,
In hut or court, nowhere we meet,
  A house so dear as childhood's home.

No other guard's so true and kind
  As arms of mother, clasped secure;
Where sheltered innocence may find
  A love so tender and so pure.

The maiden fair and bright-eyed boy,
  The household pets and father's pride,
Will never feel so keen a joy
  As when they climbed yon mountain side.

In all the boundless realms of space,
  Though you should travel everywhere,
You'll never find another place
  So full of peace and free from care.

Beyond the reach of bitter strife
  No hateful discords bring complaint.
Youth spends the years of blissful life
  In freaks which suffer no restraint.

While boys may yearn in age to live,
  And soon grow big like other men,
Then they would all their treasures give
  If they could play like boys again.

No prize so tempts on sea or shore,
  None lies so near the heart, forsooth,
As this rich boon, to gain once more
  Those boyish days, that home of youth.

The pleasing scene who can portray
  When gifts surprise each girl and boy,
As bent on festive holiday,
  With sparkling eyes all dance for joy?

They take more sport in doll and gun,
  More mirth in drum, more glee in fife,
More merriment and sterling fun
  Than many a man in years of life.

The baby dolls, both great and small,
　　Wear mask and dress, of diverse styles;
The children, too, are covered all,
　　Like mother's face, in wreath of smiles.

The merry children laugh and sing,
　　And naught they feel is ever sad.
In all the earth where dwells the king
　　With mind so free and heart so glad?

When man grows weary, weak, and sore,
　　His soul cries out in life's decline, —
" Sweet days of youth, come back, once more,
　　And cheer this drooping heart of mine!"

VIEWS FROM MOHAWK VALLEY.

Steep hills are decked with sheets of silvery snow,
That glisten in the sunlight's wintry glow;
Streams from those mountain summits swiftly glide,
To mingle with the ocean's swelling tide.

Along the river banks the waters flow,
Where stately elms and weeping osiers grow;
The parting clouds disclose ethereal blue,
And radiant skies delight the ravished view.

BACCHANALIAN SONG.

Naught on earth is dark or dreary,
　　Nothing sad or wrong;
All the world is bright and cheery,
　　While I tune my song.

Gay is life, replete with pleasure;
　　Hope's transcendent aim
Strews the path with plenteous treasure,
　　Proud ambition's claim.

Fill the cup from crystal fountain,
　　Till it tips the brim;
Fancies fleet, o'er moor and mountain,
　　Like wild eagles skim.

Here recline in calm composure,
　　Lest ye faint again;
Pile the board with sweet ambrosia, —
　　Food for gods and men.

Dance the Terpsichoric measure;
   Harp and viol play;
Halls of gayety and pleasure
   Greet the dawning day.

Revelry and dissipation
   All the night prolong;
These are choicest of the nation, —
   Ladies, feast, and song.

WE WILL GATHER ROUND THE FIRESIDE.

A SONG.

We will gather round the fireside with our loved ones,
  In the storms of winter, bleak, and bitter cold;
We will sing the hymns they taught us in our child-
    hood,
  And repeat the songs that never will grow old.

We will tread the measured cadence of the music,
  When we hear the strains of harp and violin;
We will catch the joyous spirit of our boyhood,
  And recover the same form that we have been.

Oh, let strains of glad rejoicing now refresh us,
  While we sing the ditty of our endless youth;
And we make the welkin echo all around·us,
  To the praise of hopeful love and knightly truth.

Let us ring the cheery bells, and strike the cymbals,
  For our life is glad and merry all day long;
Our companions, too, are lively, gay, and jovial;
  And they join us in our hearty notes of song.

Take the cup which not inebriates, but cheers us,
   And then drink the health of kind and friendly guest;
When the draught and song shall make it light, to please
      us,
   We will add the cheer of blithe and mirthful jest.

Let us pledge ourselves to friendship in the beaker,
   Filled with sparkling water from the crystal spring;
When our cups are flowing, brimmed with cheering
      nectar,
   Like the gods, we'll sip the liquor while we sing.

SAD TIDINGS.

Softly the night wind sighs
  Through hollow pines afar;
Darkness broods o'er the skies,
  Nor beams a single star.

Calmly the forest bends
  Beneath the swelling breeze;
The woodland spirit sends
  A dirge through moaning trees.

The gale which sweeps the sea
  Bears tidings o'er the hill,
Of one long dear to me,
  Whose tender voice is still.

Bent like the willow's bough,
  Crushed down with mighty grief,
This heart, in holy vow,
  Seeks, by the cross, relief.

Leans on the Saviour's arm,
    Where man may sweetly rest,
Safe from all earthly harm,
    Like lamb on Jesus' breast.

STEPS IN THE PATHWAY OF MORNING.

Through the eastern sky now streaming,
  Comes the bright, rose-tinted dawn;
Up the steep hills clearly gleaming,
  Fair Aurora leads the morn.

Forth the great sun, upward climbing,
  Scatters darkness, as a cloud;
While the morning bells are chiming,
  Earth lets fall her nightly shroud.

One by one, the stars are fading;
  Softly treads the new-born day,
All the nooks of earth invading,
  Lo! she drives the gloom away.

Nature wakens fresh from slumber,
  Wrapped in dewy mantle round;
Rich the jewels without number,
  Scattered o'er the grassy mound.

Now the lark, no longer darkling,
   Chirps her clearest matin song,
Drinks the dew-drops, brightly sparkling, —
   Earth's sweet tears, her glades among.

Man with rapture wakes from sleeping,
   Soon begins his daily toil,
Holds all nature in his keeping,
   Fells the trees, or tills the soil.

Hillsides, bathed in sunlight, glisten,
   Feathered songsters plume the wing;
Even angels stoop to listen,
   While the flocks of wild birds sing.

IN BATTLE.

Fierce as yon thunderstorm
  Fall their keen blows,
Dashing in boldest form
  'Gainst mighty foes;

See now the blazing guns, —
  Mountains of smoke!
Forward the column runs,
  Scorning the stroke.

Brilliant the clashing swords,
  Like lightning flash;
Steeds rush through knightly hordes,
  Onward they dash.

Squadrons so quick to move
  Stand at their post;
Cloudless the sky above
  That splendid host.

Loud peals of cannon's roar
   Echo again ;
Swift come the frenzied corps,
   Scouring the plain.

VICISSITUDES AND STABILITY.

While song birds chant in Heaven's attentive ear
  Their sweetest orisons, devoutly sung,
While seraphs bend, with keen intent to hear,
  In rapt enchantment, ghostly choirs among,

Awake and listen; view the spectral scene;
  The gentle shepherd tunes his rustic lay;
Forth go the flocks and herds to pastures green:
  Morn opens wide her gates to rising day.

No maid so fair as, clad in azure blue,
  The rosy morn, our subtle sense to charm;
While in her hand she brings the honey dew,
  And perfumes rich as Araby's sweet balm.

Her golden locks, replete with glistering sheen,
  Hang down in tresses, mantling o'er her breast;
Her eye, the sun, with rays of sparkling mien,
  Looks far away to reach the distant west.

Dark night, on sable wings, hath deftly flown
    To Erebus, the haunt of ghostly shades,
Where winds, with hollow sigh and piteous moan,
    Hold carnival, a-hurtling through the glades.

Thus, with the shadows, sorrow, sin, and death
    Escape beneath the rays of that bright sun,
Whose brilliant beams restore life's fitful breath,
    When Christ proclaims eternal day begun.

In olden time, hast thou not seen thyself,
    From out the heart of yonder silent wood,
The stray lamb torn, when seized by angry elf,
    And bleeding, crushed and mangled for his food?

No more substantial than the bubble, fame,
    Life rises up, while yet we gaze and wonder,
Floats through the air within its fragile frame,
    With one spasmodic throe, then bursts asunder.

Day ends the dismal night; night ends the day:
    Naught is but changes in this universe,
While all terrestrial things die and decay,
    Entailing pain for Adam's sin and curse.

What shall we find more stable and secure?
  Sun, earth, and stars together roll;
What still exists that shall for aye endure?
  Shall flames of doomsday burn them, like a scroll?

Is naught above, beneath, around us sure,
  Since all have perished in the ages past?
Yes: something still remains that must endure;
  For God and heaven eternally shall last.

THE BUTTERFLY CHASE.

INTRODUCTION.

In youth, we oft pursued the elf-like fly;
Oft chased from field to field, from flower to flower,
The bee, the humming-bird, with plumage gay,
The butterfly, till wearied in the chase,
We sought for rest and shelter from the heat
Beneath some tree, beside the babbling brook,
Where cool, refreshing shade restored our strength,
And sparkling waters quenched our burning thirst.
Transformed from worm to chrysalis, behold!
The insect mounts and flies, as beautiful
As that fair rose, on which it lights and sips
The honeyed sweetness freshly stilled in dew.

THE CHASE.

Just watch him now, while we pursue
Over the meadows all wet with dew!
Hurrah! hurrah! oh, see him fly
Above the trees, along the sky!

See how he skims the azure blue,
Like a skiff that sails the waters through!
How he rises up and soars on high!—
Now wait a minute and he'll come nigh.

We'll hurry on, both you and I,
And catch the swift, bright butterfly,
And when he drops near me or you,
We'll trap with caps as children do.

Over the hill and over the dale
He fans the air with his purple sail.
He shoots right upward, then dashes down,
And skirts close by the steepled town.

He floats like a bubble on gentle breeze,
And lightly glides by the stately trees;
He watches for blossoms in plains below,
Spies beds of flowers as white as snow.

He's just as happy, as happy can be,
While he plunges on through his crystal sea.
When he scents the rose he will not stay,
But mocks the boys by flying away.

He sports and jumps as well as they,
And laughs and frolics the livelong day.
Merry is he as the lark that sings,
While he flits along with his silvery wings.

As pretty a thing as you can see,
The butterfly outrivals the humble bee, —
Look there he sits on the leafy vine
And sips the sweets from the eglantine.

Jump quick, and seize him under your hat!
He's a nimble mouse; be spry as a cat, —
Oh, yes, 'tis true, you've caught him at last!
Shut him up in this box and hold him fast.

How he flutters and struggles to slip away!
He pants and trembles throughout the day;
He jumps and flies with weary wing, —
Oh, loose him and let him go, poor thing!

What! hang him up in that bright show-case,
And pin his wings in its vacant space,
To show his beauty for months and years?
Nay, rather pity his cries and tears.

This tragic story draws near its end;
The butterfly loses his trusty friend, —
Within the chest in pain he lies,
His body pierced, alas! he dies.

THE FATHER'S HEROISM.

Blow on, ye piercing winds,
Your stormy torrent finds
    This spirit free:
Howl, howl, through creaking pines,
Ye bring terrific signs
    From off the sea.

Dash, mighty billows, dash;
I hear your frightful crash
    Along the strand:
Beat now against the rocks,
And send your fearful shocks
    Throughout the land.

Ye waves, that roll on high,
Toss upward to the sky,
    And hit the stars;
How can ye e'er come down?
The mariner to drown,
    From vaulting Mars.

Strike, mighty waters, strike!
Your billows all alike
    Wash on the shore:
Ye dreadful storms, increase;
Your terrors never cease,
    Oh, nevermore!

I see the lightning's flash,
I hear the thunder's crash,
    Terrific roar:
The floating form of wrecks,
The broken spars, and decks,
    Lie on the shore.

Hark, hark, I hear a cry;
Some sailor passing by
    Utters a moan;
Some boy, in deep distress,
Implores our helpfulness,
    By that loud groan.

Come, help, he may be mine, —
Press quickly through the brine,
    Rescue and save:

Alas! it is my son, —
It must be bravely done,
    I'll breast the wave.

Boldly he ventures in,
A human life to win,
    With bated joy;
If haply he may save,
From th' oceanic wave,
    His drowning boy.

Palsied in every limb,
He strives in vain to swim,
    O'er waves so high;
They toss him back to land,
Where both upon the sand
    Now breathless lie.

Heroic unto death,
They spend their latest breath
    In deeds well done:
Thus in each other's arms
They rest from earthly harms,
    Father and son.

THE SINGING BIRDS.

Ye blithe and merry birds that sing
  So prettily on yonder bough,
So sweet your cheerful voices ring
  That Heaven records your morning vow.

Your music floats o'er dale and glen,
  So many a weary heart to cheer;
It echoes back from groves again,
  And charms the sense of all who hear.

Like Orpheus' golden lute of old,
  That song attracts all creatures wild:
It tames the lion brave and bold,
  Subdues the panther as a child.

Still twitter on, resplendent choir,
  And let us hear your choicest songs;
No other voices can aspire
  To rival yours in all these throngs.

I love to listen while ye sing
  Those tuneful numbers, soft and sweet:
What rapture and delight ye bring
  To loving friends, as oft we meet.

Were I a bird, to humbly crave
  A branch and nest upon this tree;
An ecstasy of joy I'd have,
  Forever near you thus to be.

Oh! how it soothes the throbbing brain,
  And cheers the drooping, gloomy heart,
To list to that melodious strain,
  And in that song to bear a part.

Give me the music of the birds,
  As nature teaches them to sing;
Their song is sweeter far than words,
  Or on the tree, or on the wing.

Their notes are wild, as are the woods,
  Within the forest, where they build;
Their tones are weird, as are the moods
  Of sense and feeling, there instilled.

The wise man looks beyond all these,
  And kens the Maker of them all,
And his Creator strives to please,
  Who notes each sparrow and its fall.

The just man searches moral laws,
  And judges 'twixt the right and wrong,
Discerns the Author and First Cause,
  And thanks Him for both birds and song.

PRESENTIMENTS.

Our dreams are oft realities foreseen,
  Or premonitions of some future thing,
Or records else of deeds long past and gone,
  Or tales, forsooth, of acts now on the wing.

In visions waking, seers of old foresaw
  The vista stations of the coming years;
As hills and mountains on the landscape seem,
  Or as the range of distant stars appears.

The prophets were but dreamers full inspired,
  With clear afflatus of celestial things;
And poets are none else than vision seers,
  Who drink the deepest from Pierian springs.

OUR MOTHER.

————

O'er all the earth, by land and sea, we roam,
  And wander by the mount and on the wave;
Return at last to view our childhood's home, —
  The saddest spot of all is mother's grave.

As oft we kneel beside the earthy mound,
  And there bedew with tears the sacred sod,
While round we scatter flowers upon the ground,
  Our comfort is, we hope she dwells with God.

If ever patience could all grief endure,
  Hers seems like Heaven's forbearance from above;
Was man's affection ever sweet and pure,
  There's none that equals our own mother's love.

No friendship's half so warm, so kind, so dear,
  As mother's, which we fondly hope to share;
All else so hollow, hers is so sincere;
  And naught so tender as a mother's care.

Fidelity of woman, oh, how strong!
　In bearing every ill without complaint:
It lasts through every bitter, burning wrong,
　And meekly welcomes many a sad restraint.

Time mellows sorrow by the lapse of years,
　But loss of mother we must mourn for aye;
No limit can assuage the flow of tears,
　For ages cannot purge our griefs away.

Our mother's grave with holy thought inspires;
　What sacred musing fills the hallowed place!
Within, our hearts enkindle glowing fires,
　When memory recalls her beaming face.

Who can disdain her love? or who forget
　The gentle touch of sympathy she gave?
No other greeting that we ever met
　Could equal mother's, were she queen or slave.

Dear mother! shrine of all the graces given
　Where we may worship, and yet blameless be;
With fond idolatry approved by Heaven,
　We cry to thee, we kneel, we pray to thee.

To thee we offer votives of our love;
  Before thine altar, incense burn in prayer;
We pluck the flowers from vernal field and grove,
  And wreathe thy form with garlands sweet and fair.

ONCE.

Once every minute a new heart throbs,
   Another infant cries;
And mundane mortals have their sobs,
   Fresh pleasures and new sighs.

And once as oft some weary soul
   Flies on immortal wing;
Some human spirit seeks the goal,
   Where saints and angels sing.

One life each moment wings its flight,
   Beyond the Lethean shore,
Or enters realms of darkest night,
   And will return no more.

Once every hour the village clock
   Rings out the time of day;
The hands move on, as if to mock
   The dalliance of delay.

Once every week we doff our clothes,
    Put on our Sunday best,
And enter church for sweet repose,
    And claim our Sabbath rest.

Some go there only to be seen,
    And some to sleep and nod;
Some fondly dream, with mind serene,
    And others worship God.

So oft the Journal comes to hand,
    Its columns we peruse,
And "Once a Week" lies on the stand,
    Replete with startling news.

Once in a month the moon is full,
    Then softly dark and pale;
She waxes, wanes, grows bright or dull,
    Till endless changes fail.

Once every year the roses bloom,
    And once they fade and die;
The old year to the new gives room,
    Whose glory passeth by.

Once birds fly off to warmer climes,
　　And once return to build;
Leaves, grass, and flowers decay betimes,
　　With blasting tempest killed.

The mermaid princess once a year
　　Bathes in her native sea;
Renews her youth and beauty there, —
　　Immortal queen is she.

The sun glides through his cyclic course,
　　A meteor flashes by;
The Earth regains her fertile force,
　　Responsive to the sky.

Our race is born once in an age;
　　We act the dream of life,
Fulfil our part, then quit the stage,
　　And shun this mortal strife.

Once in eternity Heaven's throne
　　Is set on crystal sea;
Man stands before his God alone,
　　His soul forever free.

Once in a day the sun appears
   And sinks below the west;
We rise with mingled hopes and fears,
   Then toil and stop to rest.

When morning spreads the twilight ray,
   We hail the gilded sky;
We sleep and waken once a day,
   As once we live and die.

The morn of life dawns on us bright,
   Its evening sends us sleep;
Death draws the curtain of the night,
   While all around us weep.

Eternity will have its dawn, —
   The sleep of death shall break;
Blest is the soul which then is born,
   When buried saints awake.

"Wake, sleep no more," the angel cries —
   "No more, thou earth-born soul;"
"Wake, sleep no more," all heaven replies,
   "Thy life hath reached its goal."

THE PROCESSES OF NATURE.

With midnight darkness join the noontide glare;
   Thus, blending deftly, all extremes may meet,
To dazzling glory adding gloom's despair;
   With winter's chillness mix midsummer's heat,

When ice and snow, hail, sleet, and pouring rain,
   Commingling in the stream of motley form,
Thus disappear, and soon return again,
   Steam, vapor, cloud, and mighty thunderstorm:

So through the current streams of human life
   The warm blood courses from its spring, the heart;
Corpuscles, red and colorless, in strife,
   To eye and cheek their beauteous tinge impart.

What varied elements their strength combine
   To blanch the lily and to paint the rose;
A million essences these plants entwine;
   Ingredients numberless their barks enclose.

Thus Nature's process works in all her spheres,
  Developing from primal parts the whole;
Inanimate, endowed with life appears;
  Immortal man, from earth, a living soul.

AMBITION'S DUTY.

'T is noble to depict the lovely dawn,
　Or paint the glories of a sunset sky,
To tell to ages that are yet unborn
　The verities of life that will not die;

But grander still to banish human fears,
　To welcome to our homes the wandering swain,
With tender zeal to watch the sick girl's tears,
　And minister to bodies racked with pain.

Through heat of summer's sun, and winter's cold,
　The struggling poor must toil or sadly wait;
The last possession must be quickly sold,
　The wife and children driven from their gate.

Your generous heart may help, your hand may guide,
　May lead them to some shelter bright to cheer;
Your counsel bring them to their Saviour's side;
　Your sympathy may dry a starting tear.

THE HUNTED STAG.

The wild-wood here no trace of man can show;
   Until this day, indeed, no daring swain
Hath traced his footsteps in the driven snow,
   Nor scoured the bounds of yonder neighboring plain.

The sportive hunter wakes the rosy dawn,
   And sips the nectar from his pearly shell;
He calls his pack of hounds with blast of horn,
   And ventures forth o'er mountain, crag, and dell.

The ancient savage, on his trackless way,
   Pursues the fallow deer through forest hill;
While belching bloodhounds hold the stag at bay,
   The burnished arrow's aimed with archer's skill.

The point is deadly, as his eye is true,
   The bow of sapling ash as strong as steel;
The sunlight flashes from its dome of blue, —
   Nought from his vision can the mark conceal.

Five summers gone, the deer first saw, too soon,
   His antlers mirrored in the sylvan stream;
So many winters since the changeful moon
   Revealed her image to his youthful dream.

Just as he stoops to drink from crystal spring
   He hears the yelp of dogs approaching near:
The startled woodland birds refuse to sing;
   The fleetest of the forest pricks his ear.

Full forty paces range their heights apart,
   From hunter's station to the panting deer;
Straight-aimed toward centre of his trembling heart
   The arrow-head of flint seems doubly near.

He shakes his antlers with defiance bold,
   And tosses up his head with spirit brave;
Must his warm life desert his body cold?
   O huntsman, prithee pity him and save!

Yea, spare the creature that thus dreads to die!
   Give ear one moment to my earnest plea!
If thou must kill him, wilt thou tell me why?
   Hath not one God created him and thee?

The spirit of the beast, who is that knoweth?
  Let no fell weapon rend that life away;
The spirit of the beast that downward goeth, —
  Help him, O Heaven, that precious current stay!

The cruel huntsman draws his bow-string back
  With all his force, the utmost stretch to gain;
Lets fly his arrow through its pathless track,
  Nor heeds one instant all that creature's pain.

Trembling at first, the stag leaps by one bound;
  He starts to run, but soon is brought to bay;
He reels and totters, quickly circling round,
  And falls to earth at length, man's captured prey.

Toward yonder hut, on burdened shoulders borne,
  His long, last journey ends without a tear;
To grace his captor's banquet, rent and torn,
  In death a prize to furnish human cheer.

OUR MAY-DAY SONG.

Sing we merrily in spring time of this genial month of
    May,
While the blossoms in the meadow pour their perfumes
    through the day;
Hear the birds upon the treetops chirp their sweetest
    roundelay,
"Listen to our festive music, 'tis our bridal song,"
    they say.

Hark! the pretty robin twitters, his notes sweeter than
    the rest,
While he coos unto his helpmate, as they build their
    straw-thatched nest;
Song and toil they aptly mingle, till the sun sets in
    the west,
Breasting every anxious struggle, trust they always for
    the best.

Perch they cheerily, while building, on those boughs of
    oak and pine,
Musing haply of their nestlings in those leaves of
    vernal vine,

While in fancy thus their ringlets circling round them
    they entwine, —
In our harassing endeavors, would their joy were only
    mine.

Care they never for the morrow, since the fields abound
    in food,
Thus their Heavenly Father feedeth them with bits
    so nice and good,
Covers them with downy plumage suited to their humble
    brood, —
Oh, how sweet, in voice so trustful, thus to speak their
    gratitude !

From these native forest warblers we may learn our
    lesson true,
Even birdlings with their singing teach us much we
    ought to do;
Let us build our houses gladly, cheerful labors still
    pursue ;
Since we've gifts more rare by nature, we will praise
    God's blessings too.

FAIR MAY.

Greetings of love to this merry month of May!
   She visits banks where everglades grow fair:
Crown her with garlands, blossoms wild and gay,
   Twine violets midst tresses of her hair.

Through autumn's blast and dreary winter's cold,
   She hid within her rocky cave the while,
Till, rested and refreshed, with aspect bold,
   She comes with sunny face and cheerful smile.

Adorn her brow with fillets of sweet flowers,
   O'er her fair sisters still she reigns their queen:
Make ready soon her arbors and her bowers,
   Shout her glad praise through fields and meadows
      green.

Down by the brooks, where purple pansies blow,
   We hail Queen May, whose beauty never fades,
Along the shores where gentle streamlets flow,
   Where sweet arbutus trails in woodland shades.

See her come tripping o'er yon distant hill;
   Thrush, lark, and bluebird spread the joyous wing,
And chant their lays with rustic pipes so shrill,
   Vying the shepherd's song with notes of spring.

With fairy wand she smites the plastic ground,
   And bids the garland fruit trees scent the air;
No spot so lone but violets are found,
   Which scatter odorous perfumes everywhere.

The bellowing kine that in green pastures graze
   Call to their trustful young so often lost;
The genial sun pours down his welcome rays,
   And vernal dew supplants the wintry frost.

Forth to the field the ploughboy spurs his team,
   And turns the sod in furrows deep and wide,
Then sows his seed; nor doth he seldom seem
   The master of that land which forms his pride.

New lives in myriad forms spring forth in May,
   Bird, insect, beast, and worm, creep, run, or fly;
Nature hath varied scenes, rough, wild, and gay,
   Whose spectacle of wonder towers up on high.

THE SOWING AND THE REAPING.

Fair is the grain where we may trace
  The products of the loamy ground,
But fairer still the fruits of grace
  Which in the human soul abound.

The kernels sown in richest sod,
  Produce the crops in sums untold,
So beareth fruit the Word of God,
  Some thirty, sixty, hundred-fold.

Be ours the work to plough and sow
  And cultivate immortal soil,
Then fields of golden fruitage show
  Prospective guerdon of our toil.

THE POET'S PLEA.

Say, Mr. Editor, wilt thou have a poem?
If it doth not suit you, then you'll throw him
Into the basket underneath the table,
Where you may stow the poet, if you be able.

This is the poetry of early spring,
And I assure you it is just the thing
You want to fill up your first, leading column,
And I tell you truly, the words are very solemn.

'Tis pity, since I'm such an able poet,
That no one else but me should ever know it.
My poem's just a trifle over-florid,
Compared with which all else is simply horrid.

"No room," you say? then you can salt it down;
Long keeping will give it great renown,
And, though it may become a trifle stale,
It will give your big paper a Buncombe sale.

I' ve read your wretched paper heretofore
And always praised it, though it was a bore;
Until you once refused my rhyme on squirrel,
Which when my best girl read it made her ill.

I had ten volumes of your paper bound,
And when the folks came in I passed them round,
Thus advertised your pesky sheet. In turn
Publish my poem, or they all shall burn.

I' ve been put off too many times before, —
I tell you I' ll not stand it any more ;
If you do n't publish it without delay,
I'll thrash your miscreant self this coming day.

— Peter Whitcomb.

LIFE'S PHASES.

Hushed to silence, fast asleep,
  Lo, the babe has ceased her cry;
Smiling features, dimples deep,
  Mark an angel passing by.

Then she wakens from her slumber,
  Laughs and offers love's sweet kiss;
Frolics, gambols without number
  Tell us of fair childhood's bliss.

Age and wrinkles, stooping form,
  Bending body, crippled gait,
After years of pelting storm,
  Do this infancy await.

Lights and shadows interweaving,
  Joys and sorrows, pleasure, strife, —
Make the morning and the evening
  Of this bright, sad, cheery life.

PSALM OF DESTINY.

Where are those hopes of my earliest childhood,
    Joined with the dreams of my youth?
Buried in shadows by streams of the wild-wood,
    Fast by the fountains of truth.

Where are the friends that so oft I was greeting,
    Treasured in garners above?
Lost to the eyes that once gladdened their greeting,
    Torn from our hearts' warmest love.

Where shall I sleep when the twilight is fading,
    Deep in the darkness of night?
Soon shall the trumpet, my slumbers invading,
    Welcome the morrow's glad light.

Question the cloud-winds, the stars' mystic shining,
    Whither those spirits have fled:
Answers returned from creation combining;
    " Resting in silence," they said.

Ask ye the host of archangels their story,
 Veiling each face with their wings;
"Each sainted soul," they said, "lives still in glory;
 Gladly in triumph he sings."

Hear Thou the prayer that Thy servant now saith, Lord ;
 Conquer my sin and my pride:
Lighten mine eyes, that I sleep not in death, Lord,
 Thou art my Shepherd and Guide.

TO MISS MAY.

Sweet hope lights up the face where one may see
   The winning smile. Oh, couldst thou hear me say
How deeply yearns my eager heart for thee,
   My gentle May, my own dear idol, May!

The modest blush that tinges thy fair cheek
   Betrays within a noble, spotless soul,
Chaste as the virgin moon, whose beams so weak
   Far o'er the earth spread joys from pole to pole.

One gentle touch from thy soft hand hath wrought
   The tender passion in my inmost heart,
And Cupid lingering in thine arbor caught
   Hath won my ear with tales of magic art.

Both day and night I'll dream of thee, and when
   The shadows fall across life's turbid stream,
I 'll lay me down to quiet rest, and then
   To sleep, until I share love's sweetest dream.

List! 't is the thrilling voice of love I hear
   Which stirs my soul with some strange mystic power,
From o'er the lake creeps in my ravished ear
   Like heaven's sweet song in this still evening hour.

Here on this mossy bank I'll now recline,
   In this enchanting scene spread on the shore,
Bathed in the light of stellar suns that shine
   From heaven's blue dome, — oh, bliss! I need no
     more.

Beneath this Druid temple's holy fane,
   Rear up the altar for this heart of mine,
The heart that craves a queen's benignant reign
   And pours libations o'er her sacred shrine.

NO MORE NIGHT.

How lovingly the sun, with his bright beam,
   Has kissed the sloping side of this fair bank,
Where blue pied violets bordered the stream,
   As oft the lowing kine strayed here and drank.

Once, canopied in mist, the verdant hills
   Stood bathed in sunlight after showers of rain;
Their summits crowned with fragrant daffodils,
   Surpassed the loveliness of Sharon's plain.

The splendid lustre of that brilliant cloud,
   Which shows her scarlet blushes in the west,
Speaks her glad summons to the toiling crowd;
   Calls weary beast and man to home and rest.

All nature shares the evening's calm repose,
   While summer twilight slowly fades away;
When life's brief span shall reach its destined close,
   How sweet shall be the peace which ends that day!

The twilight of that eve, however bright,
  Shall fade in deep, dark shade and solemn gloom;
And then, enshrouded in death's dismal night,
  This corse shall sleep within its narrow tomb.

But oh! what gladness, on that glorious morn,
  When, waking, we behold eternal day;
When crowns and diadems shall e'er adorn
  That ghostly form which never can decay.

The full duration of that endless day
  No man can measure and no mind conceive,
Whose joy and beauty never pass away,
  Which has no gloom, no night, no sombre eve.

THE SICNARF FANTASY.

A MEDLEY.

Since first the daylight dawned upon mine eyes, —
    When life began, with all its hopes and fears,
Through what entrancing scenes along these shores
    My bark hath glided on, full sixty years!
Oft have I watched the starry heavens at night,
    In wonder lost, with strange, mysterious air;
Whence came those countless orbs, endowed with
        light, —
    So vast, so grand, magnificently fair?
Could you, my comrade, trace with me once more
    The outlines of the land, the sea, the sky;
Could we but sail along that native shore,
    Where tidal joys in hearts of youth dashed high, —
'Twould bring the memories of golden days,
    And all our visionary hopes restore.
Against my breast the throbs of impulse beat,
    Like waves against the ocean's rock-bound shore.

Oft in the storm, in frost and winter's cold,
   We've breasted well the blast, when northern winds
Have chased the clouds away and cleared the sky,
   As sprite-hands tear the veil from gloomy minds:
And when the summer's sun has poured hot rays
   Upon this parched and thirsty soil, how oft
Have we reclined beneath the grateful shade
   Of yonder spreading elm, that towers aloft
Above the murky clouds.
   Remembrances of days long past and gone
Now crowd upon my mind and charm my soul;
   My swelling heart, with yearning all its own,
Pants for one page of memory's treasured scroll.
   I learned philosophy in Wisdom's school, —
Nothing to hate or mourn but sin, no face
   Of mortal man to fear, but only God,
All foes to overcome by His rich grace.
   We skimmed along the coast of that broad sea
Where myriads sleep, lulled by the mermaid's shell,
   Waiting those forms we fancied hovering o'er, —
In circumambient air their spirits dwell.
   Thus crowds press thickest round me when alone;
With multitudes are no companions near.
   The friends that most I love stay far away,

Whose presence serves my solitude to cheer.
  Oh, could I, like the ancient seer, behold
The future offspring of Time's pregnant womb,
  Like Hebrew prophet or Chaldean sage,
I'd haste to unravel from the tangled loom
  What Clotho, with her distaff, and Lachesis,
Have intertwined with craft and cunning skill.
  Sages have told us days of youth are best,
And we shall never share in joys more true,
  But future years will reap the harvest sown
In life's glad spring time, gleaning pleasures new.
  The moralist advises man to be
Less conscious of himself, of others more;
  Content thyself in being what thou art,
With aspirations after richer store

AMERICA.

America, my country, my dear home,
  As tendril of the vine clings to its tree,
So cleaves my heart to thy bright, sunlit dome;
  As son his father loves, so love I thee.
Land of gigantic mountains, trees, and streams,
  Where dwell heroic men in field and town,

No other land in all my wildest dreams
   Can reach thy matchless beauty and renown.
The needle's point turns to north polar star,
   Which guides the sailor o'er the trackless sea;
That beacon light upon the hill from far
   Shall draw my yearning spirit back to thee.
While drifting homeward through wild wind and storm,
   My bark may wander from the pathless way;
Love's constant vigils watch her spectral form,
   Where beckoning lighthouse casts a cheerful ray.
When peaceful shepherds hear of war's alarms,
   We see thy hills arrayed in bristling steel;
When danger threatens, calling men to arms,
   Our country's roused in might with cannon's peal;
Swords from their scabbards leap, and sabres clash,—
   The tramp of men and horse afar resounds.
Through ranks of hostile hosts our heroes dash;
   Our foes lie scattered o'er these battle grounds.
No warlike trophies match the arts of peace;
   But trade and commerce, with their busy hum,
Products of farm and mill yield their increase, —
   Fabrics from shuttle, loom, and spindle come.
A hive from which flies forth the honey bee,
   To gather sweetness from each blooming flower,

Seems but the workshop's symbol, where we see
  Mankind display the greatness of his power.
Save in the public hall, where blatant voice
  Denies the God who made us, where proud man
His own destruction seeks with reckless choice, —
  Religion, Heaven's best gift, reveals her plan
To mortals living, that for sin must die;
  And incense on ten thousand censers burns, —
The murky perfumes, curling upward, fly
  To Heaven's gate, whence answer sweet returns:
Child of my patient hope and thoughtful care,
  How oft with tender watchfulness my love,
Embracing thee, would fain thy griefs to share, —
  Send to thy troubled breast my peaceful dove!
Hail to the land of festive mirth and song!
  Luxurious viands spread their tempting hoard,
Music and jovial story cheer the throng,
  Peals of gay laughter circle round the board.
Woe to the hapless wretch that steeps his sense
  In dark forgetfulness with wine's abuse!
With beverage that spares no innocence, —
  None but the toper dares defend its use.
Thrice cursed the winebibber, cleric or lay,
  Who fosters habits of excess in wine,

Whose teaching and example lead astray
  The youth of this fair land, both yours and mine.
With sparkling wit, rich joke, and humorous jest,
  Good fellowship for breeding makes amends;
Kind Charity welcomes her grateful guest, —
  In gleeful merriment her banquet ends.

HAROLD'S ASPIRATION.

Come, gentle maiden, mistress of sweet love,
  Sit by me 'neath this shade, near this green brink;
Hear how the woodland minstrels sing above,
  Mark how these warblers rise on high and sink.
The cheerful lark thus tunes his mellow song
  And thrills his pretty mate with note so sweet.
How tender is the voice amid the throng
  Of songsters thus saluting as they meet.
Didst thou not hear the pigeon softly coo,
  Nor watch the maiden bird her lover greet?
Could I but learn from him the art to woo,
  Thou wouldst my passion with like ardor meet.

Oh, could I twine the tresses of thy hair,
　Within thine arms one blissful hour repose,
Admire thy beauty, exquisitely fair,
　And fan thy cheek that blossoms like the rose!

MY LARAMIE.

A SONG.

My Laramie, my Laramie!
　How swift the feet that tramp the town,
So thick with dust, so wild and free, —
　Thy visage gnarled with angry frown.
O Laramie, O come to me!
　I'll smooth those furrowed wrinkles down.
Do thou consent my guest to be,
　And all thy pensive sorrows drown.

My Laramie, bright Laramie,
　On trampled lawn dance by the moon;
Encircle now this poplar tree,
　Keep step in time with merry tune;

Dance, dance with me, my Laramie,
  The spirits gay will vanish soon,
And leave behind both you and me
  To slumber well this afternoon.

Come, fly with me, O Laramie,
  O'er hill and dale, afar from here;
Come trip along down by the sea,
  Where breezes blow, no billows fear,
Where swells the main on stranded lea,
  'Neath boundless realms of atmosphere;
Thy cradle rocks the brownies flee,
  Drop now to sleep, my choicest dear.

BERTRAM'S LAMENTATION.

Now I'm sitting by the seaside on the shore,
  Where the wild and raging waters far resound;
While the billows still are heaving breakers o'er,
  And the dashing waves are leaping with high bound;
And the mighty, swelling torrents fiercely pour
  So the sea-gulls kiss the wave-crest hovering round.

I'm lamenting my misfortunes evermore;
　Like the flood, my tears are falling on the ground;
Not a tittle dost thou love me, Eleanore,
　And my wretchedness no plummet lead can sound;
So my heart is pierced and bleeding, still and sore,
　There's no balm to reach the gash or heal the wound.

THE REALM OF NATURE AND OF MAN:
THEIR DESTINY.

How fair this earth appears, in robe of green,
Where busy life displays her wondrous powers,
And nature shines in beauty all her own,
Her bosom decked with garlands of sweet flowers!
How firmly stand the hills! how swift the brooks,
That from those summits gush to babbling rills,
Glide on through meadows towards the stormy sea,
Mingling sweet streams to swell the ocean tides!
When we behold earth's splendor, who would dare
To summon gray-haired prophets to foretell
That all her pride shall perish, beauty fade,
Her brilliant day sink in eternal night?

Who now would dream that princes, titled dukes,
And kings must die, their thrones and kingdoms fall,
The noontide of their brightest glory, veiled
In obscurity, must hide in darkest gloom?
Once mighty hosts were by their sceptres swayed,
But soon the lustre of their crowns must fade;
With clashing sabres ringing by their side,
They mounted high-bred steeds, prepared for war,
And trampled streets with hoofs through clouds of dust.
There once puissant kings their castles built,
And raised on high to heaven their battlements;
Beneath the shadow of their cloud-capped towers
The ancient walls of feudal chiefs still stand
In grim display, to mark heroic days.
Let not the mockery of scorn or hate
Disdain those battles or those monuments,
Which stood of yore the pride of chivalry.
Then rose the knights to majesty of state
Equal to kings. They won historic fame;
The lordly manor of both duke and prince
Stood on the hillside to be viewed from far,
With gates thrown wide to welcome stranger guests.
Then Hospitality, with festive cheer,
Spread bounty on her board fit for the gods.

Such deeds of prowess as they once performed
Surpass the records of the Greeks at Troy,
So oft their halls rang to the clash of arms.
In the blest thraldom of his nuptial bower
The proud king sits in majesty at ease,
And summons vassals to his courtly hall,
And bids them speed through yet untrodden paths,
For thrones of kings shall topple to their fall.
His heralds swift upon fleet horses fly
To wrest the coronet from royal power, —
Chivalric knights of vengeance to his foes,
That filled his spleen with cruel, murderous hate,
Can sturdy moulds of clay withstand their thrust?
The march of empire westward we may trace;
Full nineteen ages, each one hundred years,
Since angels sang the birth of Christ upon
The plains of Bethlehem; thrice these and more
Shall come and go, in ages circling round,
Till angels sound the reveillé so shrill
That mortal man shall wake from death to life.
Born from the womb of Mother Earth once more,
These bairns shall gaze upon the light of heaven,
Dwell in God's house — celestial residence.
In anguish of a mother's travailing throes
The Earth shall greet her splendid, new-born race, —

Her myriad offspring's resurrection morn;
Her lofty towers shall tremble to their base,
The palaces shall topple, turrets fall;
Her ancient halls shall quake, her elements
Of ocean, air, and land melt and dissolve, —
The smoke of their consuming fire ascend,
And naught but ashen heaps shall then remain
To mark the orbs that circled through the sky.
Their orbits tenantless shall stay for aye;
All animate, terrestrial creatures die.

THE SOUL'S APPEAL.

Eternal Father, hear Thy children's cry, —
　　Pity our sinful weakness and forgive!
As oft we stumble in the path, draw nigh;
　　Lift up our drooping hearts, that hope may live.

Our wills are weak, our purposes infirm;
　　We raise to Thee our suppliant appeal, —
Thine is the might to strengthen and confirm,
　　And Thine the skill to soothe, to bind, to heal.

When, crowned with folly which we oft deplore,
　　We sink to vices that we dare not name,
From foul disgrace to virtue pray restore,
　　Almighty Maker of this sordid frame.

When earth shall fade and mortals sink to rest,
  Ere twilight darkens and bright stars arise,
Kindle the hope within some anxious breast
  To reach the sunlight of heaven's cloudless skies.

PARADISE.

Land of fair hills, clad in immortal green,
  Gardens of Paradise, grow bright with flowers;
While from the sky, o'er this enraptured scene,
  Fragrance and beauty drop in gentle showers.

Cities and mansions built of precious stones,
  Terraced with turfs that spread through verdant leas,
All border on river banks surmounted by thrones;
  Swift streams flow by them into boundless seas.

That misty cloud which veils the golden throne,
  And hangs suspended over yonder skies,
Shall vanish, like the shades of darkness strewn
  Across the earth when morning sunbeams rise.

Ethereal spirits cluster round their king;
  Within those halls they chant their Eden song;
With silver tones their clarion voices ring, —
  Hark! hear the matins of that ghostly throng.

SONG OF SERAPHS.

Light from heavenly glory beaming
    Dawns upon this spirit land;
Radiant beauty, softly streaming,
    Cheers our mystic choral band;
Wild and weird the tones of greeting,
    Far resounding from above,
Presages of joy repeating,
    Fresh from cloudless realms of love.

Wide we spread our fleecy pinions,
    Mounted high on cloud and wind;
Sail aloft through heaven's dominions,
    Round our brows the wreaths entwined;
Dash along in regal splendor,
    Swift as fiery chariots, roll;
Borne through skies on breezes tender
    Homeward towards the shining goal.

(*Enter Ariel, who summons the assembly.*)

ARIEL'S ADDRESS.

Hail Paradise!   Immortal minions, hail!
Ye that from ancient Horeb late have come,
From Judah's mighty tribe, from Zion's hill,
Where streams gush forth in fair Siloam's pool,

Rest from your journey; gather on this bank,
Where Eden's river flows beneath your feet
Towards yonder glassy sea.   'T is well ye come;
Take greetings from the messenger of God,
Who dwells beyond Orion's distant stars,
Beyond the Pleiades, and rules on high,
Where dawns the morrow of a brighter day.
The hoary peaks of high Olympus spread
Above the sky, and, circling round their head,
The mantle of gray mist o'ertops the crown,
Like shade of mystery on realms divine.
The myriads who survive the wreck of time
Pass through these confines toward the gates of heaven.

The World, which once was young, has now grown old;
Like man in dotage, she's lost her hoary locks;
Now, bald with age, and sightless, toothless, lame,
With cane in hand, she halts and limps upon
The border of her grave.
O wondrous God! wondrous eternity!
How doth He hold the past, and future things
Which are not now, within His hollow hand,
And mold the everlasting hills with rocks
That form their base — foundations deep and strong.

Ages roll on; He still remains the same.
How fickle and inconstant is the sea!
At first a calm and placid surface, smooth,
Unruffled, like a mirror firmly set;
Till, all at once, fierce comes the pelting storm,
And those tempestuous waves, lashed by the wind,
Fret, toss, and rage, with fury uncontrolled.
The ever-shifting scenes of earth thus change;
The mariner who guides his fragile ship
Across the treacherous deep, and hears the roar
Of billows breaking in the crested wave,
Sighs for his native land, that peaceful shore
Where wife and child await his coming home.

THE WEDDING FEAST.

See azure sky, with cloudy pillars hung;
See orient sunbeams decking the eastern hills;
See the brightest path of dawn, where Phœbus drives
His golden chariot wheels, which chase away
Dark night from highest hill-tops, bringing day.
'T is Hymen, goddess of wedlock, who now comes
To sprinkle roses o'er the marriage feast,
And with her hand to garnish nuptial bowers.
Her car is trimmed with gold and softest silk;
Her tresses fair float o'er a neck of pearls;

And near her Dalliance, mistress of her train;
Her steeds, caparisoned with golden bells,
Equipped with livery of splendor, prance
With wild excitement, gayety, and joy.
She drives, in majesty of stately pomp,
Through royal highways into courtly halls,
And scatters perfumes far along her path.
Halls ring with laughter's merry masquerade,
While Prospero and fairest Una whirl
In the mazes of the giddy dance.
The footsteps of the fairies, light as air,
Keep pace with the tingling of her golden bells.
The brilliancy of dazzling light surrounds,
*And sparkling diamonds adorn her hair.
Glad messages arrive from courts and kings,
And, borne by pages tripping to and fro,
Come dainty missives, both to bride and groom,
And welcomes to merriment and marriage joy.

FAIR UNA'S WEDDING NIGHT.

In fashion most luxuriant and gay,
Soft couches in embowered arches wait
To give sweet dalliance and wedded bliss
To pairs embosomed in the arms of love.

Instantly within this moment of delight,
Outside the open casement of their room,
The sound of lute and viol fills the air
With music, charming their enchanted sense;
While the happy twain fall into peaceful rest
Midway twixt wakeful dreaming and sound sleep,
They pass the hours in ecstacy of love;
Then through the lattice creep the moonbeams pale,
To kiss the pillow whereon Una lies
Close by her bravest knight, who boasts with pride,
" Her virgin purity has met no stain."

THE MARRIAGE JOURNEY.

Nos ubi primus equis Oriens afflavit anhelis
Illic sera rubens accendit lumina Vesper.

Fling wide thy gates of pearl, thou golden East,
Let Phœbus usher in the beauteous morn.
How bright the day which follows darkest night !
How cheerful sunlight after dreary storm !
We welcome gladness when we have been sad;
Great is the pleasure after keenest grief;
Laughter is joyous after sighs and tears.

The nuptial morn begins the gladdest day,
Life knows no other time so full of joy.
The bride and groom join hands to start anew,
To walk together, side by side, till death.
Sometimes they travel over level paths;
Smooth meadows, verdant pastures now they tread.
But soon they traverse wild and thorny roads,
Again they meet pitfalls and precipice.
So, often, do they wander in the dark,
Stumble and fall while in the midst of gloom,
Or lose their way within the dismal woods.
Thus Prospero and Una, mounted in state,
Start on their way that bright and happy morn;
Thus, well equipped, they dash along the plain;
The bridal veil floats gracefully in air;
The neighing chargers champ their foaming bits
And prance and stand erect and snuff the breeze,
Display the grace and mettle of their sires.
At length the twain subdue their snorting steeds,
Ascend the distant hill far towards the west.
With reins committed to their equerry
They sink to sweet repose beneath the shade;
When lo, a rock, dislodged from off the hill,
Falls down the precipice and strikes the plain,

Revealing to their view a cavern deep,
Wherein they enter to explore the scene.
A long, dark labyrinth conducts them in,
Then, through a narrow, winding path they stray,
Till, lost, bewildered, they retrace their steps
To find the entrance closely barred with rock.
What shall they do? Where shall they flee for rest?
In vain they struggle with their prison door,
Their cries for help are heard by hungry wolves, —
There's nothing left but hopeless, mad despair.
An angel visitant, Hope, cheers their mind,
Another exit haply may be found.
They haste to find an opening far away,
Where they may once more see the light of day.
First to a land of reptiles they descend;
They listen to the solemn cricket's song;
The hiss of serpents greets their tender ears;
The buzz of asps, the fiery tongues of snakes,
Affright them with dread sights and fearful sounds.
From out the crevices of rock appear
The heads of venomous and deadly newts,
Vipers, and reptiles, with their poisonous fangs;
Then come the lairs of wild beasts, full of bones,
Replete with horrors, grim and ghastly smiles

The skeletons of men, apes, mastodons,
All strewn along the bottom of the cave, —
A pavement like the floor of hell below,
The waste and howling wilderness surrounds;
The voice of lions roaring for their prey,
Hobgoblins and chimeras dire display
Their fantasies to frighten mortal souls,
And make men shrink with fear. The lonely pair,
Now trembling, gasping for breath, and terrified,
Seek shelter in the clearer light beyond,
And enter, through a narrow gate, the land
Where witches dwell and boiling caldrons hiss;
Where human destiny is weighed with skill,
And fortune's envious wheel is rudely turned.
The twain, in listless silence, hear their song: —

THE WITCHES' SONG.

Sister, sister, gather, gather, gather round this chair;
Come from north, and come from south, and come from
　　　everywhere.
Sing together, sing together, sing around this chair;
Music sweeter, music sweeter, fills the enchanted air.

Dance, my sister, dance, my sister, dance around this
chair;

Lead the measure, beat the measure, leave the measure there;

Dance and sing together sweetly, sweetly round this
chair;

All the maidens five and thirty must their burdens bear.

Hear now our song,—
We do no wrong;
We come from far,
Immortals are.

We spirits dwell
Where none can tell;
We hasten home
When mortals come.

In darkness live;
With freedom give
The joy of night,
And banish light.

When dawn appears,
With trembling fears
And timid flight,
We vanish quite.

Now trip it lightly as ye go
'Neath shady boughs of mistletoe,
Upon the banks of Guido's stream
Where fairies sleep and brownies dream;
On pansy beds with dewdrops wet
Dance to the lute and castanet;
Keep step in tune till break of day,
Still mirrored in the moonbeam's ray,—

Light from the smouldering fernwood fire
Shall guide ye by the prickly brier.
With Jack-o'-lantern's taper bright
We'll put the spectred ghost to flight;
The spirits wandering to and fro,
Lost in earth's mazes here below,
Hearing these footsteps, soon shall flee
Down to deep caverns of the sea, —
The revelry of jocund song
Shall scatter all this motley throng.

Rise, break the spell, ghosts; mortals, listen; Rise!
Just at this instant, the queen of witchcraft turned,
Let fall her angry glance where Una stood;
Although enraged at her intrusion bold,
She dare not touch or hurt a virgin pure.
Then onward roved the twain, and fled away
Where light still brighter seemed almost like day.
The land of fairies came in view. Queen Mab
Was spinning threads of life, for weal or woe.
She scents the air with fragrant odors, sweet
As perfumes from Araby the blest; she plays
With zephyrs, tunes æolian harps, and sings,
Till the whole enchanted sphere resounds afar

With melody sublime. Her coterie
Of subjects live in spellbound ecstacy,
While graceful charms surround them with delight;
Bedecked with bright and gay attire, they shine
In plumage rich in color and display, —
In beauty rival birds of southern climes.

THE FAIRIES' DANCE.

In majesty the queen sits on her throne,
Her rocky canopy high-arching stands
Above her head. She wears a brilliant crown,
And in her hand she bears a golden wand,
Whose rapid waving to and fro commands
Attention of that fairy band, who watch
Her movements with an eager, restless eye.
She nods and beckons fairies to the dance;
Then come they, tripping over rosy beds,
Flying like birds and skipping through the air,
Swiftly pursuing, forward, backward, on
They go; they run, they skip, they hop, they dance,
Swift as a meteor's flash, the fairies fly.

Next they go on to lands of pigmy dwarfs, —
A dragon stands on guard within this cave;

Fire flashes from his eyes and from his mouth;
A dreadful, horrid creature, which affrights
Fair Una, drives her trembling back, and makes
Her shudder with the fear of dreaded death.
One gentle dwarf, more courtly than the rest,
Takes her soft hand and leads her safely through;
The dragon cowers when he passes by,
And, like a spaniel whipped, bends down his head.
Here dwell the race of Bluebeards, drenched in blood;
Bold deeds which shake the cruel powers of hell,
Make demons tremble, and cause Heaven to weep,
While angels veil their faces, — dreadful sights
And monstrous sounds are here;
Fair Una faints and swoons when she beholds
The floor besmeared with blood, and hears loud groans.

CONCLUSION.

Thus long the twain lay sleeping side by side,
With senses drugged to deep forgetfulness, —
When Una wakes to find this all a dream.

— A Fragment.

CUPID AND THE BACHELOR: OR, CUPID'S FATE.

Through a lonely path, beneath the spreading elm,
  A knightly youth and maiden stray;
Near by the shore's a skiff, with sturdy helm,
  Round which the evening breezes play.

Upon the mast sits Cupid with his bow,
  Sharp arrows crowd his quiver full;
The god of love takes aim and shoots his foe,
  But his keen weapon proves too dull.

The callous heart of gallant knight repels
  The shafts by Love so truly aimed;
The bachelor his tender passion quells,
  Nor will he benedict be named.

No brighter hue e'er crimsoned deep the rose
  Which blossoms in the hedge below,
Than blushes on that maiden's cheek that glows
  In wreath of lilies white as snow.

In doubtful contest long they sharply fight,
  Upon the stern embattled field;
Like champions proud of victors' tested might,
  Resolved perforce no whit to yield.

Love, evanescent as the rainbow's hue,
  Touched once his heart, but rested never;
Youth's passion sometime came, but quickly flew,
  Till one last call, then fled forever.

So oft Love tried again for many a year;
  Spent all his arrows, snapped his oaken bow;
O'er the sad wreck the muse lets fall a tear,
  And pens this tragedy of woe.

Where now shall Cupid seek for burnished arms
  To serve fond Passion's tender vein?
The tocsin sounds the note of youth's alarms;
  He skims the ocean's rolling main.

Like wandering Jew, he visits every clime;
  He finds no rest; spurned from each door,
Exhausted, weary, sinks before his time,
  Faints, swoons, and dies, — Love is no more.

In ages hence, when poets write their ditty,
   Still feigning how fond lovers wed
In hut, or courtly hall, or stately city,
   Then tell them plainly, "Love is dead."

'TIS SWEET TO DWELL ON SLOPING HILLS.

'T is sweet to dwell where sloping hills
   Reveal the river flowing by;
Where we may watch the rippling rills
   With sunlight streaming from the sky.

The mountain air, so pure and clear,
   Blows gently o'er the peaceful vale;
The roses scent the breezes here,
   As fragrant spices load the gale.

I love to climb the steep ascent
   Of bold Watusket's craggy brow;
With staff of sapling, rough, unbent,
   To struggle through the copse and slough.

The scene is fair, where grazing kine
   Feed on green meadows or rich moors;
Where swains transplant the fruitful vine,
   And maidens greet their rustic wooers.

The gardens which the oxen trod
　　Yield blossoms, fruitage of their toil;
Where ploughboys turned the tufted sod,
　　The sturdy yeoman tills the soil.

The busy housewife, loved and blest,
　　Around her table sets each chair;
Pilgrim or stranger, cheerful guest,
　　Finds hospitable welcome there.

Around the board the farmer seats
　　The village chieftain by his side;
The courtly squire politely greets
　　Each guest of honor, stripped of pride.

He needs no ceremony there,
　　No empty form for hearty cheer;
His manly breast and bosom bare
　　Disclose his inward thoughts sincere.

His bounty, spread with liberal hand
　　To all the poor, the hamlet knows, —
His loyalty to native land,
　　His sympathy for human woes,

Broad as the acres which he treads,
　Dear as life's vital stream, which flows
Through ruddy cheeks in crimson threads,
　Shall serve until night's curtains close.

THE REFRAIN.

'T is sweet to dwell where sloping hills
　Reveal the river flowing by;
Where we may watch the rippling rills
　With sunlight streaming from the sky.

SONG OF THE MAGPIE.

Here go I now, in my fancy free,
Skipping about like a busy bee,
Sipping the honey from bud to flower;
Dancing a jig in my lady's bower;

Hopping along on the apple-tree limb,
Chirping the song of my idle whim;
Merry and gay, like the woodland elf,
Peacock's bright feather, that's proud of itself.

Jingle the bell, with a magic spell;
Play a sweet tune on the cockle shell —
Music whose cadence these notes will prolong,
Rival the cricket's monotonous song.

MARY.

O Mary, the wife whom my bosom holds dear,
  Whose image is worshipped at God's holy shrine,
The name which forever my soul shall revere, —
  How blest was the day when I claimed thee as mine.

Beloved as a mother, a sister, a friend,
  Well treasured in store on fond memory's page;
Who dares to deny, till eternity's end,
  Thy record of virtue will man's envy engage.

Oh can I forget the deep love of the maid
  Who gave her sweet life as a guerdon to me?
Nay, rather I'd part with the world's gay parade,
  And launch my frail bark upon Death's stormy sea.

My heart has been sore since the day that she died;
  Henceforth 't is my vow, that no boon shall I crave,
But to cherish her name till I sleep by her side,
  United at last in the bonds of the grave.

SONNETS.

THE HIGHER CHOICE.

Aude hospes contemnere opes.

'T were better to be wise than proudly rich,
   Learned than fond of sportsman's affluent ease;
   Far nobler is it on our worn-out knees
The pallid cheek to kiss, in some lone ditch
Where wounded soldiers slake their thirst, from which
   They suffer pain, than our vain fancy please
   With phantoms of delight, that when we seize,
Like Sodom's apples, crumble, and some witch
   From Endor mocks the folly of our choice.
Whenever men or angels fain behold
   Deeds valiant, virtuous, lovely, they rejoice
More than at finding hidden gems and gold;
   With heart all rapture Nature tunes her voice
To hymn those glories which the heavens unfold.

FALSE SCIENCE AND TRUE RELIGION.

Infelix simulacrum atque ipsius umbra Creusœ.

'T were better choose religion when sustained
　By facts, established through the ages past
　As firm as everlasting rocks, which last
Against the tides of ocean, to restraint untrained,
Still proof against the storms of time unchained,
　Than move with every current of the blast,
　Like th' evershifting theories which cast
Disgrace on novel science so profaned.
　True science, heavenly wisdom, still divine,
Can never with religion disagree ;
　To man's great moral vantage both combine,
As chlorides with the waters of the sea ;
　With every moving particle entwine,
From foul pollution to keep them ever free.

HOME.

Ut puto, deus fio.

There never was a home so sweet on earth,
 However splendid to the world it seems,
 A thousand-fold surpassing all our dreams,
But we may find one of superior worth, —
A richer mansion, far more joy and mirth,
 Where the celestial sun bestows his beams;
 The smooth, green meadow with bright verdure teems,
Hills feel no storm, and blooming fields no dearth.
 That princely residence beyond the skies,
Hath gates of pearl, streets paved with shining gold;
 Thither my heart with eager impulse flies,
To find a dwelling in my Shepherd's fold, —
 In that abode where my dear treasure lies,
Living for ages, and yet never old.

THANKSGIVING FOR VICTORY.

Arma armans capio.

We thank Thee, O God, for all victories won
  By the force of our arms on the sea and the shore,
  Where the battle was raging 'midst the cannon's loud
    roar,
And the ship o'er waves rolling 'neath the flash of the
    gun,
While the smoke of the powder veiled the face of the
    sun.
  We remember those heroes, though we see them no
    more ;
  All their virtues we cherish, and their valor adore ;
Thus our hearts proudly foster the brave deeds they
    have done,
  When our bold seamen stood 'neath the enemy's fire,
'Midst the flying of bullets and the bursting of shell.
  Oh, how then did remembrance their courage inspire !
So many still living, though some nobly fell.
  To thank Thee, O God, is our country's desire,
With this hope, that in future days all will be well.

THE NATION'S CROWNING GIFT.

Dic hospes Spartæ.

Rich are the treasures which a nation holds,
   Within the compass of two ocean bands,
   In houses, goods, men, industries, and lands, —
Wealth which this wide, vast continent unfolds,
While this republic's destiny it molds,
   So long as our grand capitol yet stands;
   Nor can be buried in the desert sands,
Nor frozen in the frigid arctic colds.
   Well may she toss her head with modest pride,
As justly comparable to ancient Greece
   In wisdom, knowledge, wit, — her peer beside.
My countrymen, bid sad misgivings cease;
   E'en though all blessings else should be denied,
Hold War's bequest, world-honored, meek-eyed Peace.

EPHEMERAL FAME.

*La gloire est la dernière passion du sage; c'est la chemise
de l'âme.*

Thou dream, as unsubstantial as a cloud
   Whose shadow vain Ambition swift pursues,
   To gather gold from her bright sunset hues,
Soon wrapped in darkness as with nightly shroud.
O Fame, how oft thy voice proclaims aloud
   The vanity of all these fading views!
   Which print thy praises in soft evening dews,
Witnessed a moment by the gaping crowd.
   First as a vapor chilled to hoary frost,
She lies on earth unseen throughout the night,
   And in the morning sunbeams soon is lost;
So worldly glory fades from human sight, —
   Her value reckoned far below its cost,
When sages view it in true wisdom's light.

THE CHRISTENING OF THE SHIP.

Tell me what name befits so proud a craft,
 Which launched forth from the dock, upon the day
 When heaven and earth's creation snugly lay
Within the lap of chaos, weird and daft;
Till from her moorings some strong wind could waft
 Her form across the deep abyss, away
 Towards yonder haven, 'midst the ocean's spray,
Bearing rich freightage in her hulk abaft —
 The cargoes of a million nations — wrecked
Upon the coast or shoal of isles sublime.
 See how with flags of every land she's flecked!
O mighty master! sing the poet's rhyme;
 Dash thy brimmed tankard, sweet with chaplets decked,
Against this vessel; name her, Ship of Time.

THE SHELTER OF OLD AGE.

Fallentis semita vitæ.

Who then shall tend us with a sister's care,
   When our weak frames are bent with hoary age,
   And our crooked forms appear upon life's stage,
To act our part, our burdened years to bear?
What hand shall part these locks of silvery hair,
   Whitened with four-score winter's frosty rage?
   Or smooth this wrinkled brow? Who shall engage
To shelter these frail limbs from noontide glare?
   What venerable oak shall cast her shade
Across our path, when we, with crutch in hand,
   Shall lean, for strength's support, upon the spade
Which digs our grave out of the loamy sand,
   While on the dial of our years, each blade
Of grass counts one, to score what figures stand?

HESPER'S HOUR.

Μονόχρονος ἡδονή.

This is summer evening in the month of June,
 When the peaceful shadows cross the bank and stream,
 And the scene grows suitable to the poet's theme;
As the choristers of earth and air attune
Vesper carols to the wan and crescent moon,
 Which demurely casts her soft, empyreal beam
 Down through valleys, where the sleepers idly dream,
In life's eventide which shades them all too soon.
 This is peace, — calm, tranquil, sweet and silent peace.
Well befitting close of sorrow's toilsome day.
 From earth's turmoil, oh, how blest to gain release!
To be hopeful in this prison house of clay, —
 Darkling tussock, sombre grave, to find surcease
From all pain, in quiet rest 'neath Heaven's mild ray.

MINSTRELS OF THE GROVE.

Listen to the birds a-singing
  On that linden tree;
How their mellow song is ringing,
  Gladly, wild, and free!
O'er the tree-top gently swinging, —
  Only look and see
How the bluebird, lightly winging,
  Skims in wanton glee!

From his heart, with gladness welling,
  Comes that crystal song;
All his joys in concert telling,
  'Midst his feathered throng,
His gay bosom proudly swelling,
  Merry all day long;
On that oaken bough, his dwelling
  Stands secure and strong.

Hark ye while the linnet twitters
  Sweetly round her nest,
Brooding o'er the fledgling litters
  Where she seeks no rest.

Plumage in the sunlight glitters
　Bright upon her breast;
Briskly round her young she flitters,
　Fostered by their guest.

Swifter than a cassowary
　Flies across the sea,
Borne upon the wind-swept wherry,
　Oft comes back to me
This sweet carol, song so merry,
　Chickadee dee dee;
Bobolink on dappled cherry
　Sings tu-whit tu-wee.

LEGEND OF THE MERMAID.

The prince who won the mermaid's hand
   Wrote in the marriage bond this line:
"One day each year, she'll leave the land
   To plunge beneath her native brine."

She started home at close of day,
   To wonted duties on the shore;
These baths sufficed, as legends say,
   Her youth and beauty to restore.

At times 't was her accustomed style,
   With joyous heart and fancy free,
To play with Nautilus awhile,
   Her choice companion of the sea.

She thus beguiled the passing hour,
   By watching nymphs with deep concern;
Enamored, their bewitching power
   Withheld her from a prompt return.

Thus once belated, some suppose,
 She long outstayed her wonted time;
The fierce, rude winds in fury rose,
 And billows swelled to heights sublime.

Whist, ye wild Winds, and wanton Waves,
 Let Boreas with his minions sleep;
While Triton prods his vassal knaves,
 To stir the caldron of the deep.

"Oh, where is our lost princess gone?"
 In deep distress, her courtiers cried;
"Send, mighty king, Laomedon,
 To save her from fell ocean's tide.

"Haste to Charybdis, thou brave knight,
 Hesione bring safe to shore;
Search for our queen, o'erwhelmed with fright,
 Lest she may reach this realm no more.

"Go where the sirens, in some lair,
 Charm with their melody of song;
Search where Medusa twines her hair
 With serpents, 'midst her scaly throng.

"Ride on swift dolphin, safe decoy,
    'Mid dire chimeras, which the king,
Bellerophon, would fain destroy;
    With sweetest music, ride and sing.

"Oh, help us now, dear Hercules;
    This monster of the sea, compel
To grapple, and his trophy seize;
    Rescue Hesione from hell."

Thus Cerberus his conquest yields
    To victor's prowess, soon confessed;
Our sea-nymph, through her own sweet fields,
    Homeward returns, beloved and blest.

Beyond the walls of ancient Thebes,
    The Syrian king, his nation's pride,
In mausoleum calmly sleeps;
    Close by him rests his mermaid bride.

SONG OF THE FLOWERS.

Under the myrtle bough,
  Where blooms the mignonette,
Heaven hears our sacred vow,
  While we so soon forget;
The mistletoe with heather blends;
The cloudless sky around them bends.

Blazoned in civil war,
  The white rose and the red,
Badge once inspiring awe
  In foes to battle led,
Long since have faded 'neath the snows,
Kissed by each wintry wind that blows.

How dear the nations prize
  The thistle, shamrock, rose!
Each with his neighbor vies,
  To rival and oppose
This emblem of a people's pride,
Which grows upon each mountain side.

Perfume with odor sweet,
   God's gift to mortals sent;
For beauty's brow 't is meet,
   Fair woman's ornament.
The lily, to each maiden dear,
Decks bridal altar and her bier.

Their tribes, in conclave met
   To equal haughty man,
With rain and dews were wet,
   While Folly laid their plan;
They chose the bramble for their king, —
We could not well their praises sing.

Their monarch now, the rose,
   Fragrant in beauty rare,
With Wisdom's voice they chose,
   So bright and debonair.
Ye nations, gather hand in hand;
Shout, dance, and sing, through every land.

Hence to thy cave, black Night;
   Hide not this pretty view;
The tulip's face needs light,
   Washed with the sparkling dew;
See how her brilliant petals shine,
'Mid purple clusters of the vine.

APOSTROPHE TO NATURE.

Hail, goddess of the earth and sky!
   How dost thou hold bright orbs in hand
Release the furious winds that fly,
   Tempests that desolate the land?
Oh, tell thy reason why.

Why loose thy monsters of the deep,
   To hunt their prey 'mid broken spars
Where shipwrecked seamen dreamless sleep?
   To gorge their maws with flesh of tars,
Whose wives and mothers weep.

How dost thou teach the bird to sing?
   To build her nest upon the bough?
To hover, with her newfledged wing?
   To seek her food where farmers plough,
Where bloom the flowers of spring?

Who taught the tide to ebb and flow,
  With cunning craft and skill so rare?
The weighty answer man must know;
  Who holds the tall pine firm in air,
Against the storms which blow?

Canst thou compel the rain to fall,
  Or guide the clouds, with watchful care?
And furnish fodder for the stall,
  With those rich products earth may bear
Alike for one and all?

To fill the lap of this broad land,
  Queen of this regency divine,
Spare not to empty from thy hand
  The treasures which alone are thine,
By whom this earth was planned.

THE STRUGGLES OF AMBITION: OR, THE PURSUIT OF FAME.

Like Lucifer, from heaven he needs must fall
Who climbs the ladder to the clouds of glory,
Or wings his flight to her celestial stars.
'Tis dangerous to scale the heights of fame,
Lest he may wreck his air-ship in those storms
Which swell and rage in wild, tempestuous gust,
When his frail bark must sink to chasms below.
Lips curled in scorn, fingers with envy aimed,
Though carping critics may his bosom spare,
Shall crush his pride and shame his high-born gifts.
He starts, a youth, upon life's golden morn,
His feet still dripping with the sparkling dew;
Budding with promise, buoyed with cheerful hope,
He sips his nectar draught from mountain spring,
And journeys westward toward the gates of pearl.
Who knows how soon the wintry blast may chill,
As hoar-frost nips the first-born flowers of spring?
So perish all his earthly hopes like dreams.

No sadder sight can pain the feeling heart,
Or waken pity in the human breast,
Than to behold this proud ambition's wreck
Cast on the shore of life's most stormy sea.
The voice of envy and detraction blights,
As some sirocco, o'er the blasted fields,
Sweeps, with destructive force, life's flame to quench.
But, oh! how blest is he who dwells in lands
Where gentle monsoons blow, reviving man,
Like the sweet breath which flows from lips of praise!
Yet adulation which the world bestows
Can puff the soul with pride, only an hour;
Then his own level must each lordling find,
Or sink below it, through calumnious tongues.
Ah! what is glory, but the tinsel toy
Which some child tosses, a bubble in the air,
And mutely wonders when he sees it vanish!
Like scorpions, every breath of scandal stings;
And, while hearts sharply feel the keenest smart,
The gossips boast of the ruin they have wrought.
O Fame! how eagerly doth man's fond heart
Yearn for thee, as a mother for her child!
How difficult to reach! When found, thou art
As evanescent as the rainbow tints

Which fade away from yonder gaudy cloud.
Yet, O my soul! may fickle fortune grant
The gifts which Fate reserves for worthy minds,
To aspirants for fame, nor to those alone,
But keep some trifling token still for thee;
When Destiny, at last in that great day,
Allots his noblest prize, a seat in glory,
May a crown, at his disposal, then be thine.

"WE SHALL SEE HIM, BUT NOT NOW."

When this life's busy moments shall have fled,
And we lie resting in our gloomy bed,
Who then shall listen while the torrid breeze
Comes whistling through the branches of the trees?

When all the pleasures of this earth below
Delight those strangers whom we fain would know,
Will some fair dream in lands which we may find
Chamber its wanton action in our mind?

In some broad region of the azure sky
One figured halo stands, but draws not nigh,
The image, hallowed by a sacred vow,
Tells us that "we shall see Him, but not now."

This Son of David we shall soon behold,
The Shepherd tending His celestial fold,
Who leads His flock by cool Siloam's stream, —
Transforms to fact this promise of our dream.

(282)

AT EVENTIDE.

Sweetly to the soft note of lute, O Muse!
Celestial now attune thy monody;
Sing, while the labored ox, unyoked at eve,
Thus heavily drags his slow feet along
The dank, green pasture where his sisters graze;
Let thy smooth strain harmonious accord
With music from the curfew's chiming bells;
Teach us how calmly in his cottage dwells
The rustic peasant when cease the toils of day;
Show to our wondering and admiring gaze
The bright tints, mingled crimson, scarlet, red,
Which the skilled artist, heaven's gay, lustrous sun,
Paints on the border of Hesperian cloud,
To celebrate his exit from this day
To other hemisphere. No longer now,
As at high noon, needs man the sylvan shade,
While the tall trees their lengthening shadows cast
Across the cool, shorn glade, where lambs repose.
How quietly the peaceful meadows rest,
While the fading twilight quits the sun's lank glow!

And, as the darkness deepens into night,
The stillness into lonely solitude,
With music floating on the evening breeze,
With shepherd's pipe, and song of nightingale,
Blending their tones with music of the spheres,
The distant stars, no longer veiled by day,
Nor fearing now the sun, their tyrant king,
Who rules their brightness with imperious sway,
Come tripping singly to our firmament;
Through their long labyrinth of endless space,
To peep with curious eye through crystal discs
Bored in the curtains of the ambient sky,
And lave this earth with their supernal rays.
The soul now welcomes the dalliance of sleep,
Which wraps this tenement of clay in robes
Attractive to the idol god of dreams;
And in rapt ecstacy, behold we lands
Where wonders dwell, and fairies with their elves
Play tricks and pranks of rare astonishment.
No more can we recall till we awake,
When stars are gone, music has ceased, all sights
Have fled, like spectres seen in wonderland.
After these dreams ten thousand times renewed,
Beyond the age of four-score anxious years,

We reach the peace of life's gray eventide;
Shall we not rest in quiet, dreamless sleep?
And when the sun shall rise, with brighter beams
Than mortals ever witnessed, we shall wake
To greet the morning of eternal day,
'Mid seraph songs and angel trumpets' blast.

TO THE FATHER OF WATERS.

Flow on, thou mighty River, still flow on,
  Till all thy waters mingle with the main,
Where sails the ship, as graceful as the swan,
  To bear those fortunes which the nations gain.

Still constant may the tempest and the flood,
  Thy channel fill from tributary brooks;
As vessels from the heart convey the blood,
  So mountain creeks, their streams from welling nooks.

Flow like the current of this human life,
  Majestic waters, o'er thy bed of clay;
Thy turbid stream depicts our earthly strife,
  Thy rough and winding bank, our devious way.

In all the tracery of thy course sublime
  Thou art the emblem of man's high degree,
Whose feet, responsive to the calls of time,
  Lead to the shore of that wide, boundless sea.

Father of waters, bring us many a gift
  For towns and cities on thy favored brink
The fertile soil with enterprise and thrift
  And purest beverage that man can drink.

Like thee, fair River, ages drift away,
  Bear to their port the wealth and pride of earth,
Stored in those archives till that wondrous day
  Whose just assize shall measure their true worth.

THE TEMPLE BUILDING AND WORSHIP.

Upon the top of Zion's sacred hill,
    Where God's high altar stood in days of yore,
The quarried rock, fresh hewn with artful skill,
    Awaits the workman's trained and trusty corps.

King David here awaked his harp's sweet sound,
    With matchless beauty swept those tuneful strings,
Where now we choose this fabric's holy mound,
    And build this temple to the King of Kings.

In silence towering toward the cloud-wrapped skies,
    Through realms of air where God alone can reign,
With awe the world amazed beholds it rise,
    A temple reared, a grand majestic fane.

Within this court the first fruits of the vine
    Shall flow, libations poured for sacrifice;
The nations here shall worship round this shrine,
    The smoke of incense unto heaven shall rise.

Beneath the spreading roof, how many prayers
  By suppliant lips shall be devoutly said;
Forms bent and worn with countless earthly cares
  Shall kneel where tears of penitence are shed.

The sceptered monarch, with his stately brow,
  Must beg the blessings which his heart may crave;
While side by side, both rich and poor shall bow, —
  The mitred prelate with the humble slave.

Oh, could we know and feel each sordid frame,
  Once pure but now defaced by sin's control,
Contains an altar, with its sacred flame,
  For God's indwelling with each human soul!

The spirits there can brook no man's control,
  But they must weep for joy; nor can the throng
Restrain emotions of the ardent soul,
  Wrought into rapture by the seraph's song.

They tell us of a temple far away,
  Built from the rock on everlasting hills,
Whose pinnacles beyond the reach of day,
  Heaven's firmament of stars with radiance fills.

How blest to kneel before God's earthly shrine,
  And all our burdens to His altar bear!
May this benignant portion still be mine,
  Till I shall join in nobler worship there!

THE NIGHT.

Darkness and mystery o'erhang the night,
  When sable clouds spread out their misty veil,
And creatures grope their way bereft of light,
  In blindness searching out some huntsman's trail.

Through trackless paths of woodland, dense with boughs,
  Lost wanderers, intent to reach their home,
With eager hearts press on, and breathe their vows,
  When safe escaped, they never more will roam.

'Tis midnight where the foggy wild-wood stands,
  Deep is the silence and the darkness drear;
The sombre shades spread far to distant lands,
  And rayless gloom fills up earth's atmosphere.

Could man but hear one voice, or else behold
  One flash of light, streaming along the sky,
Content he'd grope, till orient forms unfold
  The gates of morning, where night's shadows fly.

Fit hour for deeds of violence and blood
　　Which may go free, unpunished, and unseen;
When storm-wrecked galleys sink beneath the flood,
　　No signal hoisted marks what isles between.

Dark night, most fit for quiet rest and sleep;
　　No voice nor sound disturbs our sweet repose, —
The time when many earth-born mortals weep,
　　Pray that this life of sorrow soon may close.

Night is the hour for love and fond embrace,
　　Tender caresses of the friends most dear,
Pursuits of pleasure neither mean nor base —
　　Dancing and song, with our hostess' right good cheer.

To some 't is time for revelry and drink,
　　And softer vices which we will not name;
From these all Christians must with terror shrink,
　　As vileness merits obloquy and shame.

Come, dreams of bliss, bestow those wholesome charms
　　Which lock these senses with a giant's might;
Let slumber round us fold quiescent arms,
　　And force our hearts to bid the world good-night.

THE MIGRATORY SONG-BIRD.

While winds are sighing, birds begin to sing
Their gladdest songs among the leaves of spring;
The boughs and branches, blending with the strain,
Grow vocal with that music's sweet refrain.

Whence hast thou come, fair robin, from those shores
Of far-off Hebrides or rich Azores?
Where thou hadst frugal repast, worms and flies,
Proud guest of warmer climes with balmy skies.

Through what bleak regions of the earth and air,
O'er glen and mountain, didst thou boldly dare
To wing thy flight across the arid wild,
To reach this home of nature's roving child?

Ah! why shall cruel man with luring bait,
With snare or gun destroy thy loving mate,
Thus leave thee friendless and alone to sigh,
To wander comfortless, with grief to die!

Alas! the fledglings in their lonely nest,
Still faint and hungry, plead with panting breast.
May Heaven bestow the wonted morsel craved
That broken-hearted song-birds may be saved!

Their powers so well apportioned to their need
Compels comparison with human greed;
Their privilege of travel through the air
Yields them immunity men cannot share.

In their dependence 'tis their noblest pride
That food and vesture are by Heaven supplied;
Their songs sweet music which salutes the morn;
Their wings the fairest plumes that maids adorn.

THE SORROWS OF THE LOST.

What means eternal torment of the soul?
   Remorse of conscience, which the wicked feel,
For deeds of darkness, crimes beyond control,
   Like scorpion's sting, or racks on penal wheel.

Oh, tell me what is hell? A place unprized,
   Where mind on thoughts of sorrow madly dwells;
A gracious God neglected, Christ despised,
   Heaven lost, — heart's anguish which no seer foretells.

BEINGS HOVERING IN MID-AIR.

How many spirits, on the wild waves doting,
  Are flying homeward to their native lea!
How many spectres, through the air come floating,
  Which these dull, wistful eyes can never see!

These worlds above us, of ethereal function,
  Contain inhabitants allied to man;
The atmosphere of earth, their destined junction,
  Holds multitudes in limits of a span.

When drop, at last, the scales from our crude vision,
  We gaze on space with wonder and surprise,
Survey these fields, for ages called Elysian,
  How shall we veil our dazed, astonished eyes.

Oh, could we look, with keen gaze far off reaching,
  With eyes of eagles, that can face the sun,
We might behold the witness of Heaven's teaching,
  Ere our celestial life has yet begun!

THE VESPER HOUR.

Ring, bells, ring,
 Sweet call of kirk's muezzin
  Now summons us to prayer ;
Bring, oh, bring
 The hopes of Heaven's blessing
  Borne on the evening air.

Sing, yea, sing,
 Ye choristers, whose voices
  Reach through those gates of pearl.
Ring, bells, ring,
 While earth in song rejoices
  Where clouds of incense curl.

Rise, flames, rise,
 On sacrificial altars
  Burn your slain victims trine.
Cries, still cries,
 The priest who never falters
  Before his temple's shrine.

" Alla Hu!
   Of gods there is no other,
      Come to the house of prayer,"
Sheik warns you:
   " Bismillah, Paynim Brother,
      At mosque no sandals wear."

Hark! oh, hark!
   We hear the curfew ringing,
      And choral anthems roll;
Dark, how dark,
   Night's mazy veil in swinging,
      While village church-bells toll.

All past by;
   Upon the grave's dark border
      Comes forth life's vesper hour.
Earth and sky,
   By word of heaven's great Warder,
      Shall wither like a flower.

Like young grass,
   In lonely vales of sorrow,
      When Time's long shadows fade,
Our lives pass;
   We sleep until the morrow,
      Beneath death's evening shade.

Hark, now hark,
   Celestial choirs are voicing
      Their peals, like thunder's roll;
Mark, now mark,
   How angel bands rejoicing,
      Welcome each ransomed soul.

THE SHIP OF WAR.

While through the rent cloud the red storm light is flashing,
   And the ship has to plough the rough waves of the sea,
When o'er the lone deck the wild billows are dashing,
   This heart, noble, brave sailor lad, pities but thee.

When the vessel sinks deep in the cleft of the wave,
   And the waters of ocean now threat to o'erwhelm,
Oh, where is the Power which can tenderly save, —
   Save the mariner, mighty to master the helm?

The warship rides bravely by Hatteras' shore,
  While the winds lash the sea in tempestuous gales;
She sinks, and her crew shall arise up no more;
  Her marines sleep in peace where the myrmidon quails.

By the shore of an island, within the safe port,
  In the snug, quiet harbor at anchor she lay;
But the torch of the Spaniard from the treacherous fort
  Fired the deadly torpedo, concealed in the bay.

Where now are the victims of Spain's dreadful hate?
  'T is the hate which forever scorns the sanction of law;
Is there one hero left who would challenge their fate?
  In our agony, is there one whose voice is for war?

Strike! strike for your comrades! for they need no plea;
  They who died without warning, by treachery slain;
Help the patriot Cubans, their country set free;
  Wreak revenge for the tars who manned the hawsers
    of Maine.

THE TEMPLE ON THE HEIGHTS.

In marble corridors 'neath some high dome,
Swells virgin beauty like the fragrant rose,
'Midst perfumed dewdrops of the summer air,—
In stately mansions where embosomed love
Holds converse meted to each nuptial bower,
On mountain ranges far above the clouds.
There is a temple built on hills so high
That earthly ladders cannot reach its top,
Nor bandits scale its walls to plunder gold.
Grander than any presidential manse,
Or minster on the ocean's rocky brink,
Where mighty kings are crowned in pompous pride,
Is that celestial cloister where each child
Whom God shall call His own will sit enthroned.